DRACULA

DOVER **GRAPHIC NOVEL** CLASSICS

ADAPTED & ILLUSTRATED BY JOHN GREEN

DOVER PUBLICATIONS, INC.
MINEOLA, NEW YORK

First published in 1897, Bram Stoker's *Dracula* has spawned countless films, television programs, and theatrical productions. The classic gothic novel, which begins with solicitor Jonathan Harker's journey to the remote castle of Count Dracula, provides an exciting, horror-filled glimpse into the world of vampires. A timeless favorite, the vampire theme continues to inspire a morbid fascination with these fanged, bloodthirsty creatures. More than a century after it was first published, this terrifying supernatural tale still holds readers captivated.

Although the legendary story of Dracula has been abridged here, a special effort has been made to preserve the authenticity of the narrative and keep as much of the original dialogue as space allows. The evocative illustrations enable colorists to vividly bring this compelling story to life by using crayons, colored pencils, or markers.

Bibliographical Note

DRACULA (Dover Graphic Novel Classics), first published by Dover Publications, Inc., in 2014, is a republication of the work originally published in a different format (Color Your Own Graphic Novel) by Dover in 2009.

International Standard Book Number

ISBN-13: 978-0-486-78469-4
ISBN-10: 0-486-78469-X

Manufactured in the United States by Courier Corporation
78469X02   2015
www.doverpublications.com

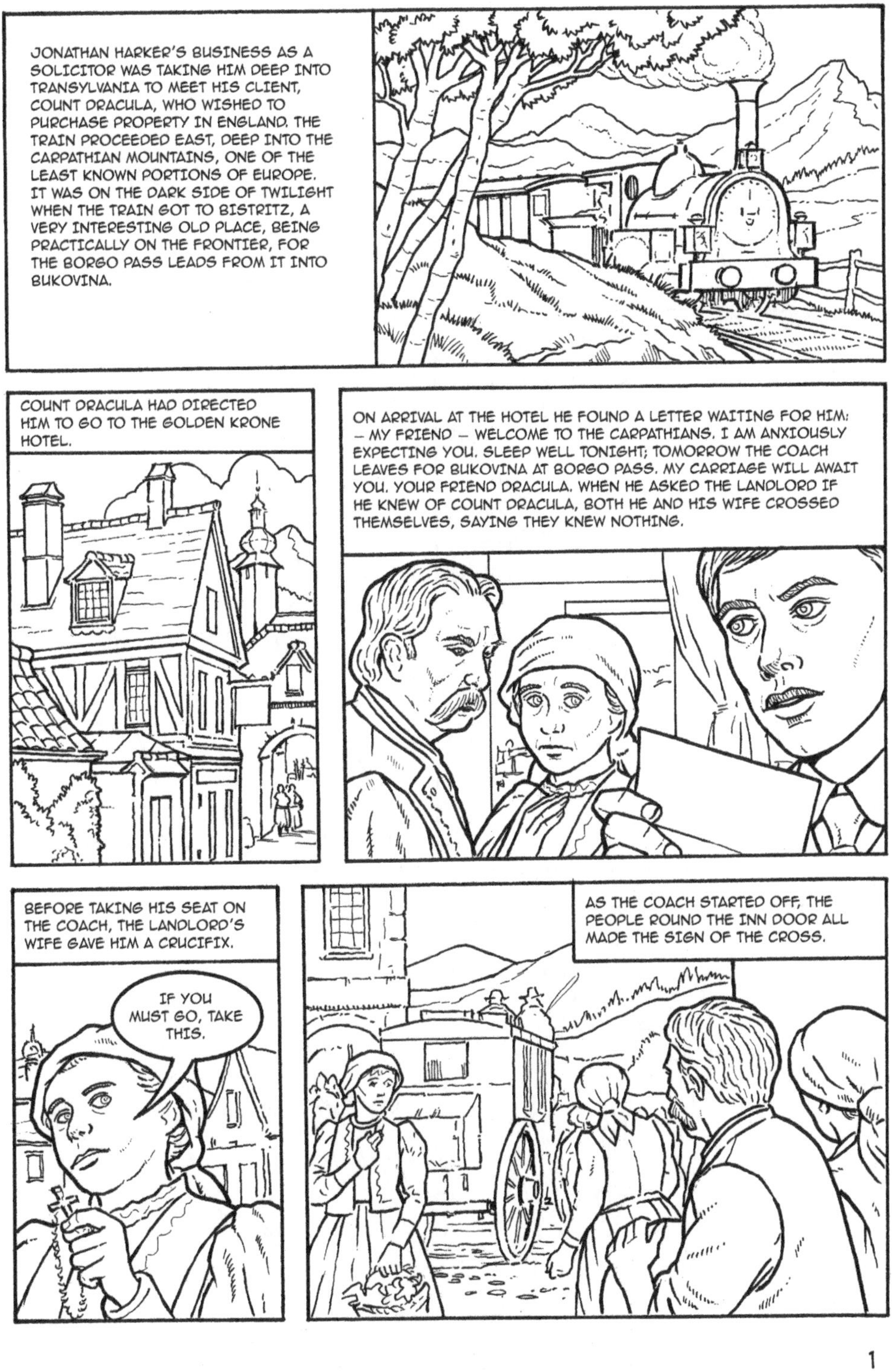

JONATHAN HARKER'S BUSINESS AS A SOLICITOR WAS TAKING HIM DEEP INTO TRANSYLVANIA TO MEET HIS CLIENT, COUNT DRACULA, WHO WISHED TO PURCHASE PROPERTY IN ENGLAND. THE TRAIN PROCEEDED EAST, DEEP INTO THE CARPATHIAN MOUNTAINS, ONE OF THE LEAST KNOWN PORTIONS OF EUROPE. IT WAS ON THE DARK SIDE OF TWILIGHT WHEN THE TRAIN GOT TO BISTRITZ, A VERY INTERESTING OLD PLACE, BEING PRACTICALLY ON THE FRONTIER, FOR THE BORGO PASS LEADS FROM IT INTO BUKOVINA.
COUNT DRACULA HAD DIRECTED HIM TO GO TO THE GOLDEN KRONE HOTEL.
ON ARRIVAL AT THE HOTEL HE FOUND A LETTER WAITING FOR HIM: – MY FRIEND – WELCOME TO THE CARPATHIANS. I AM ANXIOUSLY EXPECTING YOU. SLEEP WELL TONIGHT; TOMORROW THE COACH LEAVES FOR BUKOVINA AT BORGO PASS. MY CARRIAGE WILL AWAIT YOU. YOUR FRIEND DRACULA. WHEN HE ASKED THE LANDLORD IF HE KNEW OF COUNT DRACULA, BOTH HE AND HIS WIFE CROSSED THEMSELVES, SAYING THEY KNEW NOTHING.
BEFORE TAKING HIS SEAT ON THE COACH, THE LANDLORD'S WIFE GAVE HIM A CRUCIFIX.
IF YOU MUST GO, TAKE THIS.
AS THE COACH STARTED OFF, THE PEOPLE ROUND THE INN DOOR ALL MADE THE SIGN OF THE CROSS.

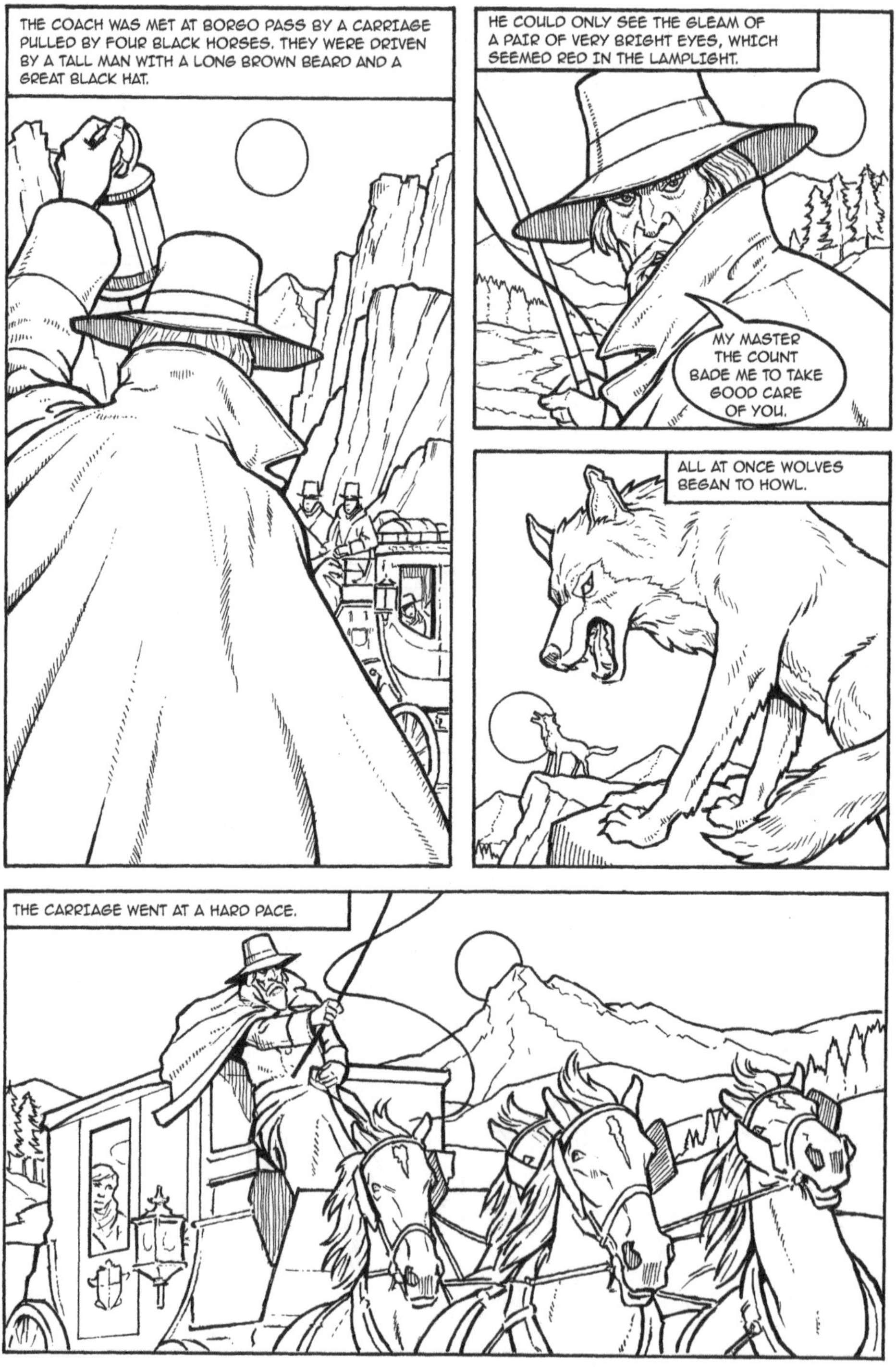
THE COACH WAS MET AT BORGO PASS BY A CARRIAGE PULLED BY FOUR BLACK HORSES. THEY WERE DRIVEN BY A TALL MAN WITH A LONG BROWN BEARD AND A GREAT BLACK HAT.
HE COULD ONLY SEE THE GLEAM OF A PAIR OF VERY BRIGHT EYES, WHICH SEEMED RED IN THE LAMPLIGHT.
MY MASTER THE COUNT BADE ME TO TAKE GOOD CARE OF YOU.
ALL AT ONCE WOLVES BEGAN TO HOWL.
THE CARRIAGE WENT AT A HARD PACE.

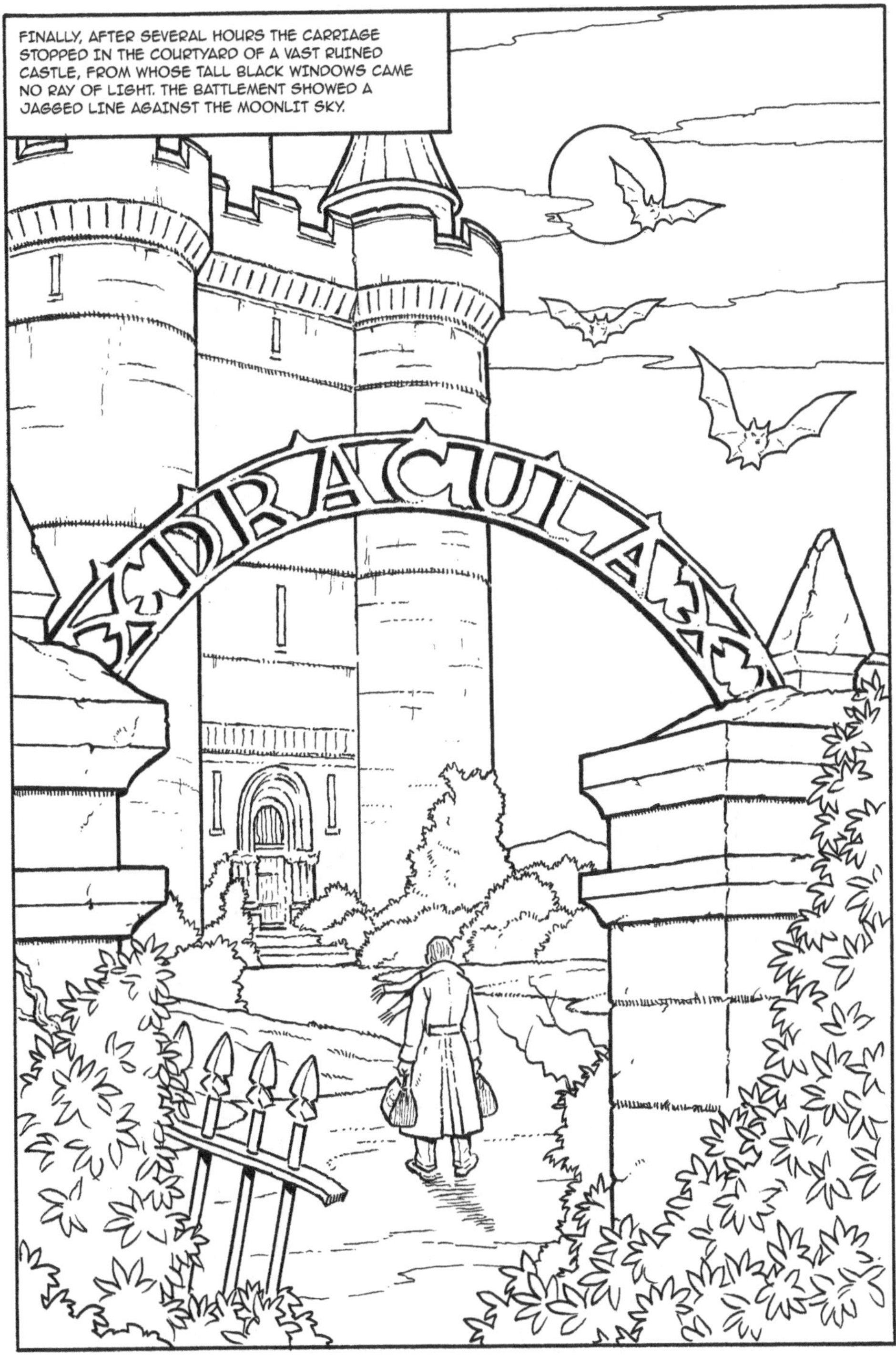
FINALLY, AFTER SEVERAL HOURS THE CARRIAGE STOPPED IN THE COURTYARD OF A VAST RUINED CASTLE, FROM WHOSE TALL BLACK WINDOWS CAME NO RAY OF LIGHT. THE BATTLEMENT SHOWED A JAGGED LINE AGAINST THE MOONLIT SKY.
DRACULA

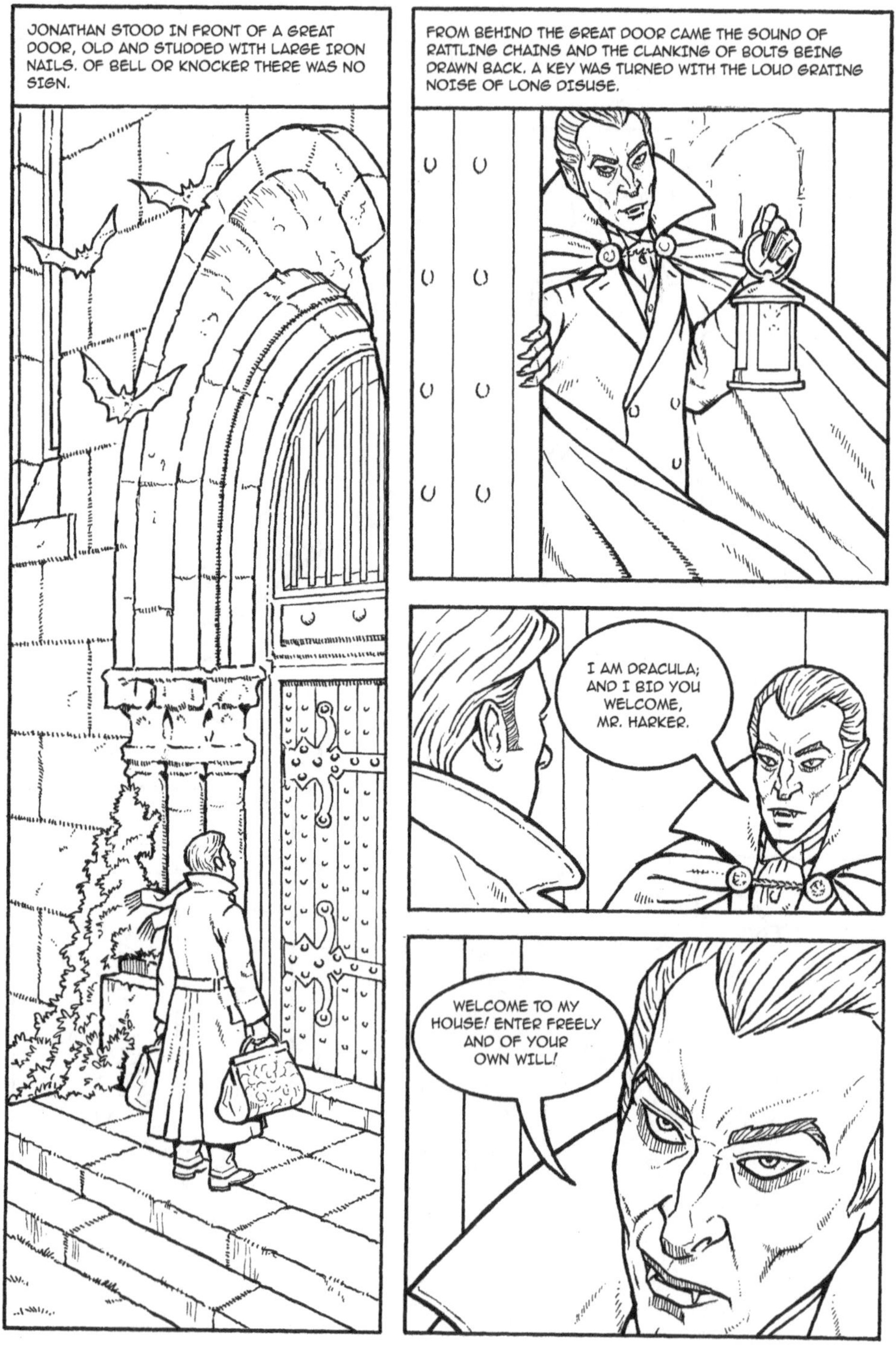
JONATHAN STOOD IN FRONT OF A GREAT DOOR, OLD AND STUDDED WITH LARGE IRON NAILS. OF BELL OR KNOCKER THERE WAS NO SIGN.
FROM BEHIND THE GREAT DOOR CAME THE SOUND OF RATTLING CHAINS AND THE CLANKING OF BOLTS BEING DRAWN BACK. A KEY WAS TURNED WITH THE LOUD GRATING NOISE OF LONG DISUSE.
I AM DRACULA; AND I BID YOU WELCOME, MR. HARKER.
WELCOME TO MY HOUSE! ENTER FREELY AND OF YOUR OWN WILL!

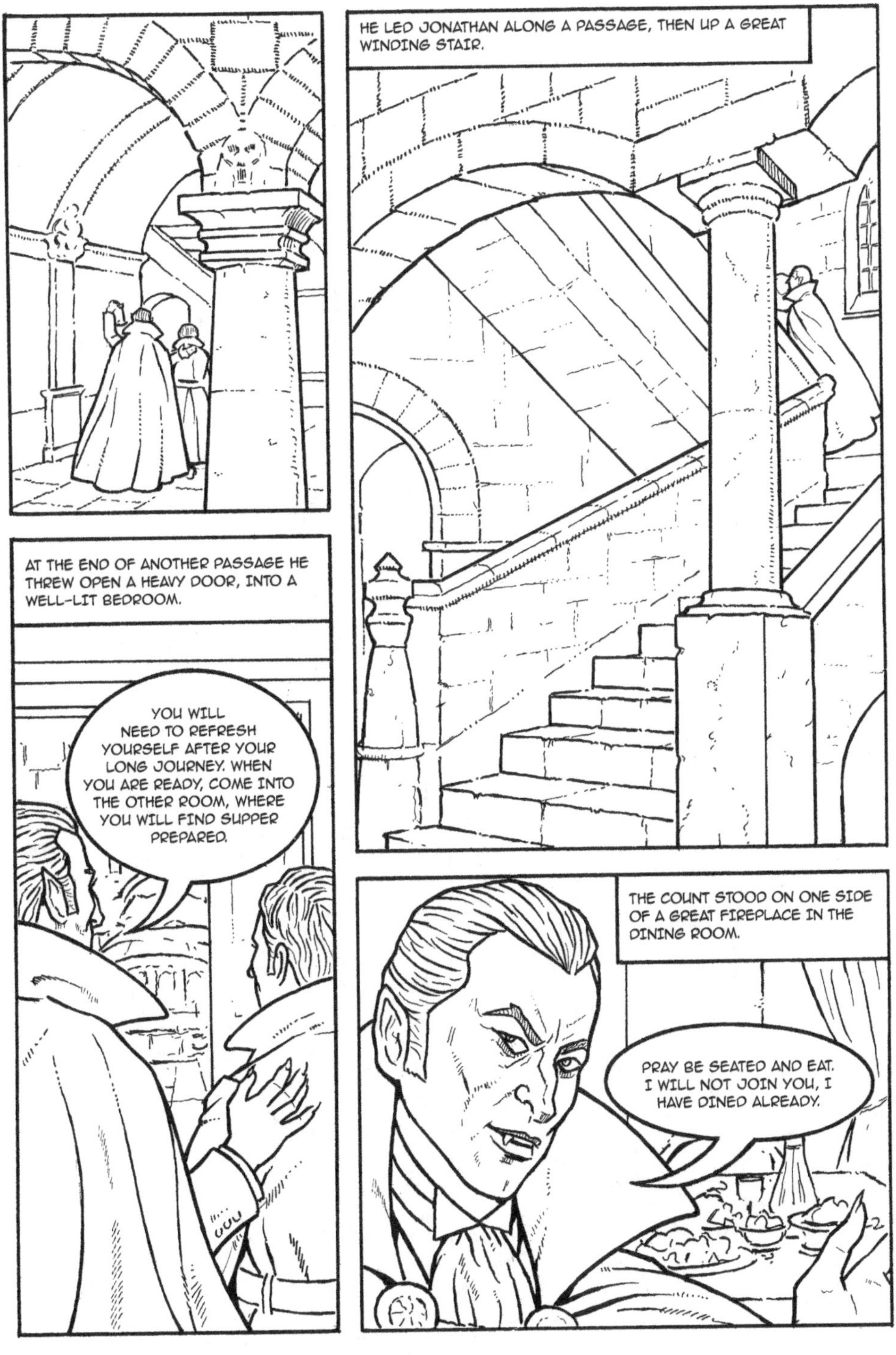
HE LED JONATHAN ALONG A PASSAGE, THEN UP A GREAT WINDING STAIR.
AT THE END OF ANOTHER PASSAGE HE THREW OPEN A HEAVY DOOR, INTO A WELL-LIT BEDROOM.
YOU WILL NEED TO REFRESH YOURSELF AFTER YOUR LONG JOURNEY. WHEN YOU ARE READY, COME INTO THE OTHER ROOM, WHERE YOU WILL FIND SUPPER PREPARED.
THE COUNT STOOD ON ONE SIDE OF A GREAT FIREPLACE IN THE DINING ROOM.
PRAY BE SEATED AND EAT. I WILL NOT JOIN YOU, I HAVE DINED ALREADY.

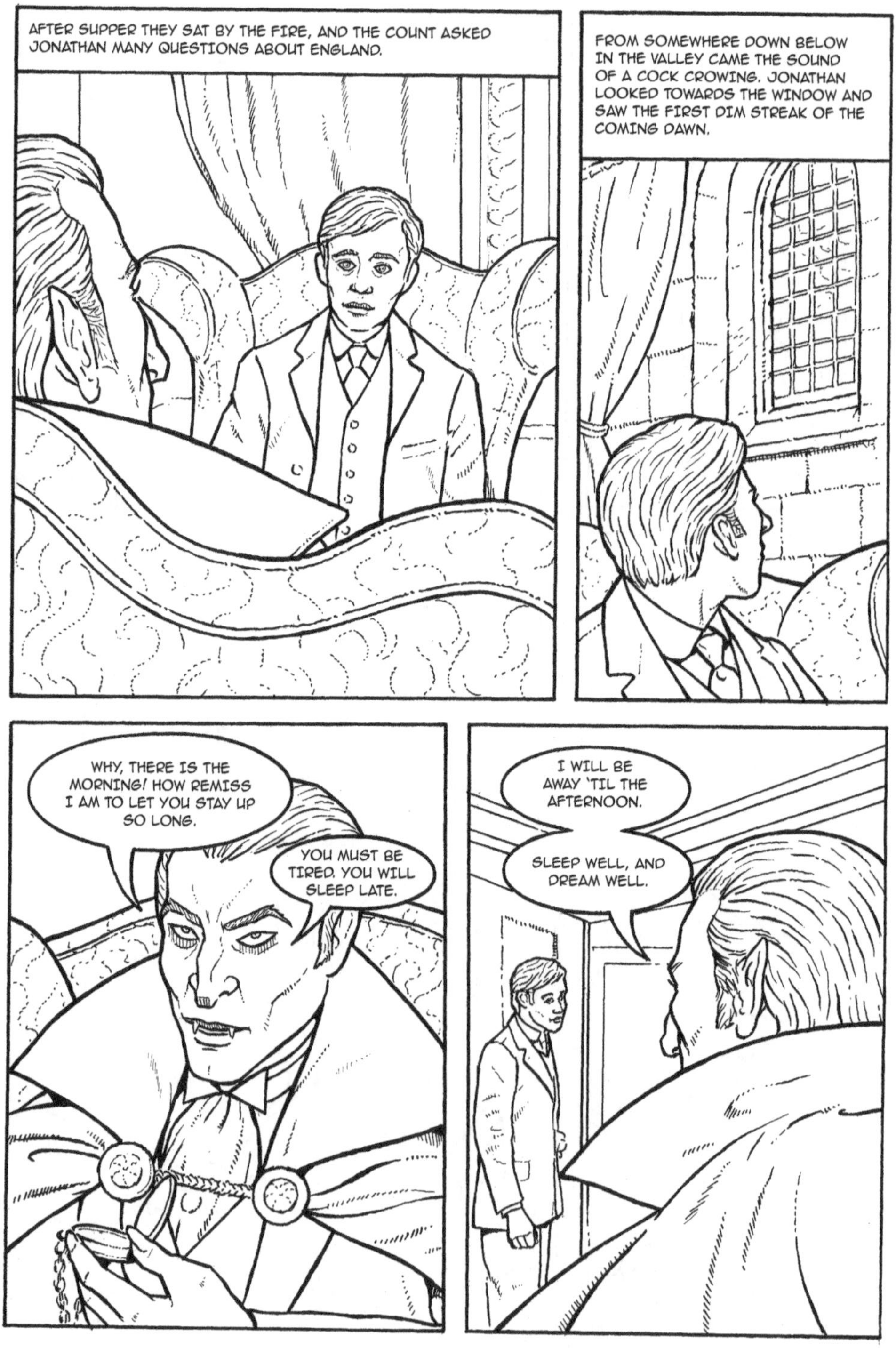
AFTER SUPPER THEY SAT BY THE FIRE, AND THE COUNT ASKED JONATHAN MANY QUESTIONS ABOUT ENGLAND.
FROM SOMEWHERE DOWN BELOW IN THE VALLEY CAME THE SOUND OF A COCK CROWING. JONATHAN LOOKED TOWARDS THE WINDOW AND SAW THE FIRST DIM STREAK OF THE COMING DAWN.
WHY, THERE IS THE MORNING! HOW REMISS I AM TO LET YOU STAY UP SO LONG.
YOU MUST BE TIRED. YOU WILL SLEEP LATE.
I WILL BE AWAY 'TIL THE AFTERNOON.
SLEEP WELL, AND DREAM WELL.

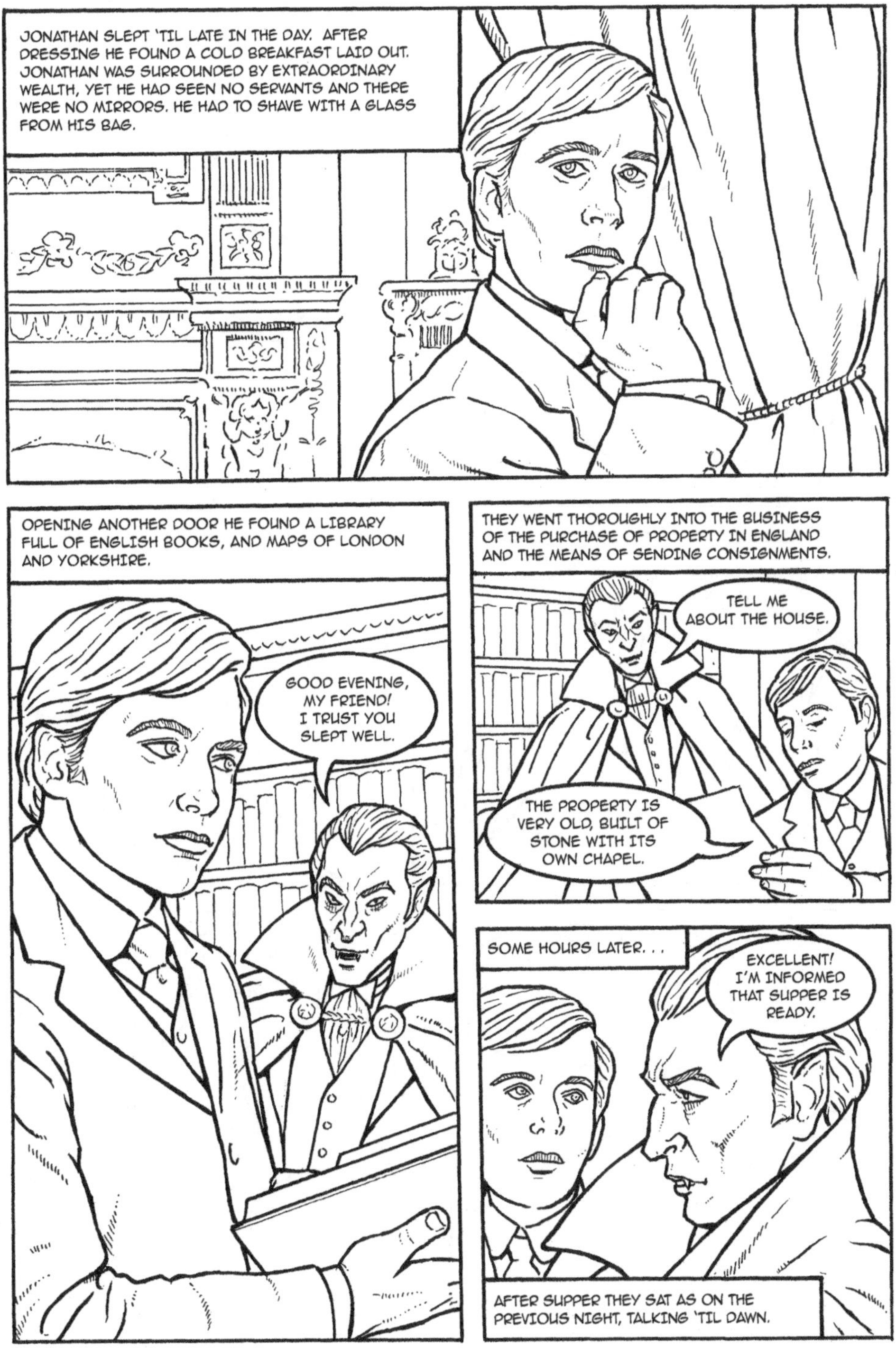
JONATHAN SLEPT 'TIL LATE IN THE DAY. AFTER DRESSING HE FOUND A COLD BREAKFAST LAID OUT. JONATHAN WAS SURROUNDED BY EXTRAORDINARY WEALTH, YET HE HAD SEEN NO SERVANTS AND THERE WERE NO MIRRORS. HE HAD TO SHAVE WITH A GLASS FROM HIS BAG.
OPENING ANOTHER DOOR HE FOUND A LIBRARY FULL OF ENGLISH BOOKS, AND MAPS OF LONDON AND YORKSHIRE.
GOOD EVENING, MY FRIEND! I TRUST YOU SLEPT WELL.
THEY WENT THOROUGHLY INTO THE BUSINESS OF THE PURCHASE OF PROPERTY IN ENGLAND AND THE MEANS OF SENDING CONSIGNMENTS.
TELL ME ABOUT THE HOUSE.
THE PROPERTY IS VERY OLD, BUILT OF STONE WITH ITS OWN CHAPEL.
SOME HOURS LATER. . .
EXCELLENT! I'M INFORMED THAT SUPPER IS READY.
AFTER SUPPER THEY SAT AS ON THE PREVIOUS NIGHT, TALKING 'TIL DAWN.

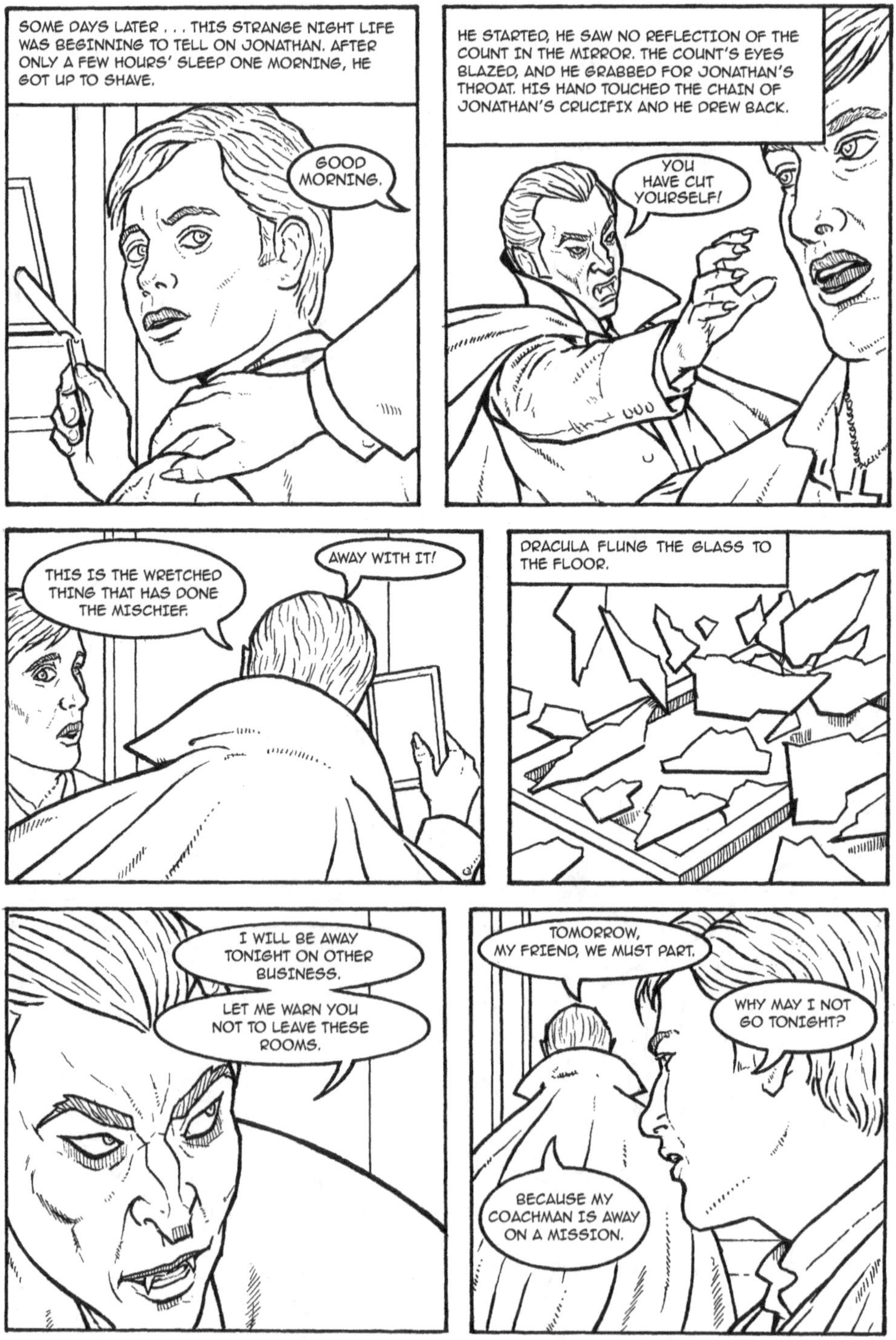
SOME DAYS LATER . . . THIS STRANGE NIGHT LIFE WAS BEGINNING TO TELL ON JONATHAN. AFTER ONLY A FEW HOURS' SLEEP ONE MORNING, HE GOT UP TO SHAVE.
GOOD MORNING.
HE STARTED, HE SAW NO REFLECTION OF THE COUNT IN THE MIRROR. THE COUNT'S EYES BLAZED, AND HE GRABBED FOR JONATHAN'S THROAT. HIS HAND TOUCHED THE CHAIN OF JONATHAN'S CRUCIFIX AND HE DREW BACK.
YOU HAVE CUT YOURSELF!
THIS IS THE WRETCHED THING THAT HAS DONE THE MISCHIEF.
AWAY WITH IT!
DRACULA FLUNG THE GLASS TO THE FLOOR.
I WILL BE AWAY TONIGHT ON OTHER BUSINESS.
LET ME WARN YOU NOT TO LEAVE THESE ROOMS.
TOMORROW, MY FRIEND, WE MUST PART.
WHY MAY I NOT GO TONIGHT?
BECAUSE MY COACHMAN IS AWAY ON A MISSION.

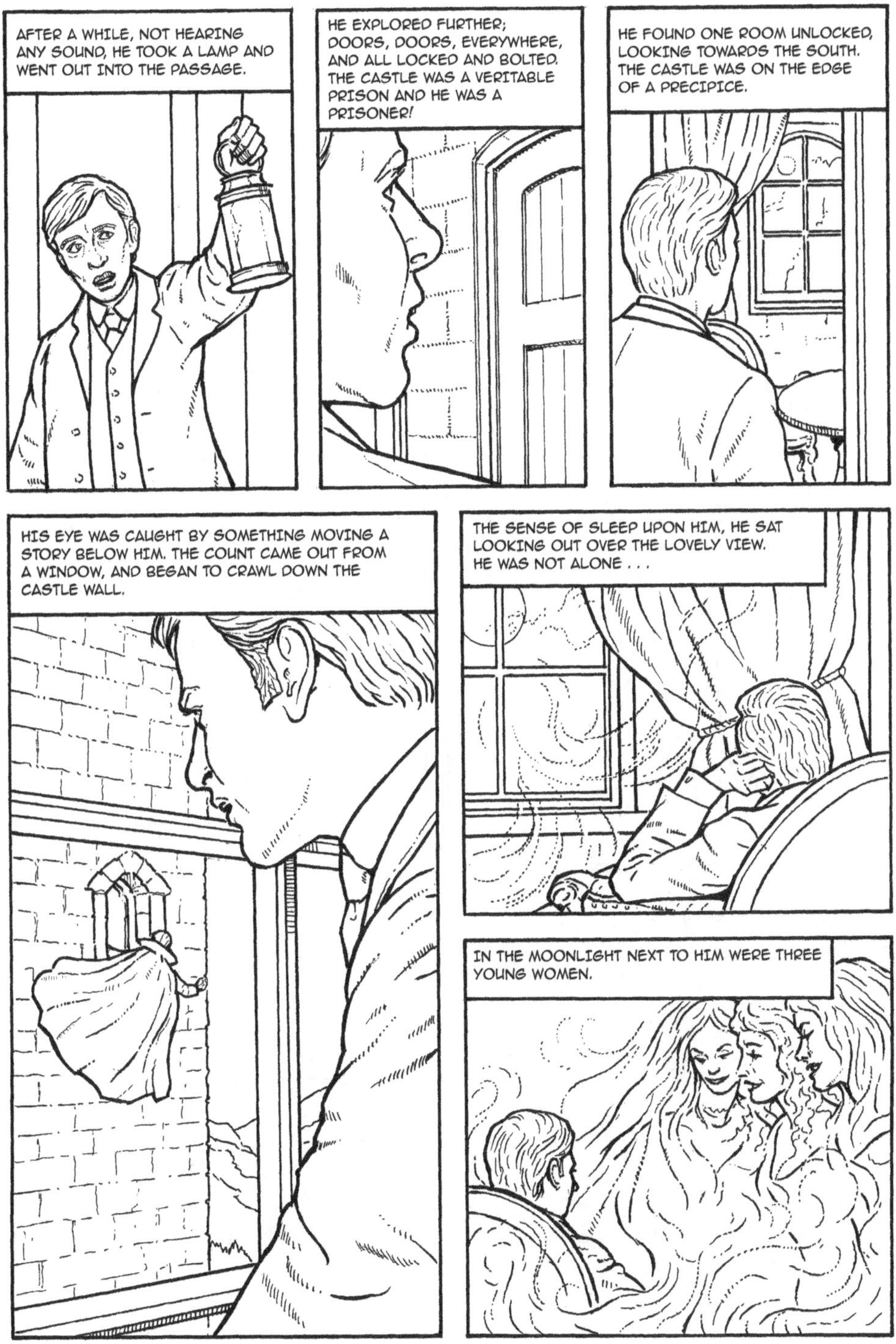
AFTER A WHILE, NOT HEARING ANY SOUND, HE TOOK A LAMP AND WENT OUT INTO THE PASSAGE.
HE EXPLORED FURTHER; DOORS, DOORS, EVERYWHERE, AND ALL LOCKED AND BOLTED. THE CASTLE WAS A VERITABLE PRISON AND HE WAS A PRISONER!
HE FOUND ONE ROOM UNLOCKED, LOOKING TOWARDS THE SOUTH. THE CASTLE WAS ON THE EDGE OF A PRECIPICE.
HIS EYE WAS CAUGHT BY SOMETHING MOVING A STORY BELOW HIM. THE COUNT CAME OUT FROM A WINDOW, AND BEGAN TO CRAWL DOWN THE CASTLE WALL.
THE SENSE OF SLEEP UPON HIM, HE SAT LOOKING OUT OVER THE LOVELY VIEW. HE WAS NOT ALONE . . .
IN THE MOONLIGHT NEXT TO HIM WERE THREE YOUNG WOMEN.

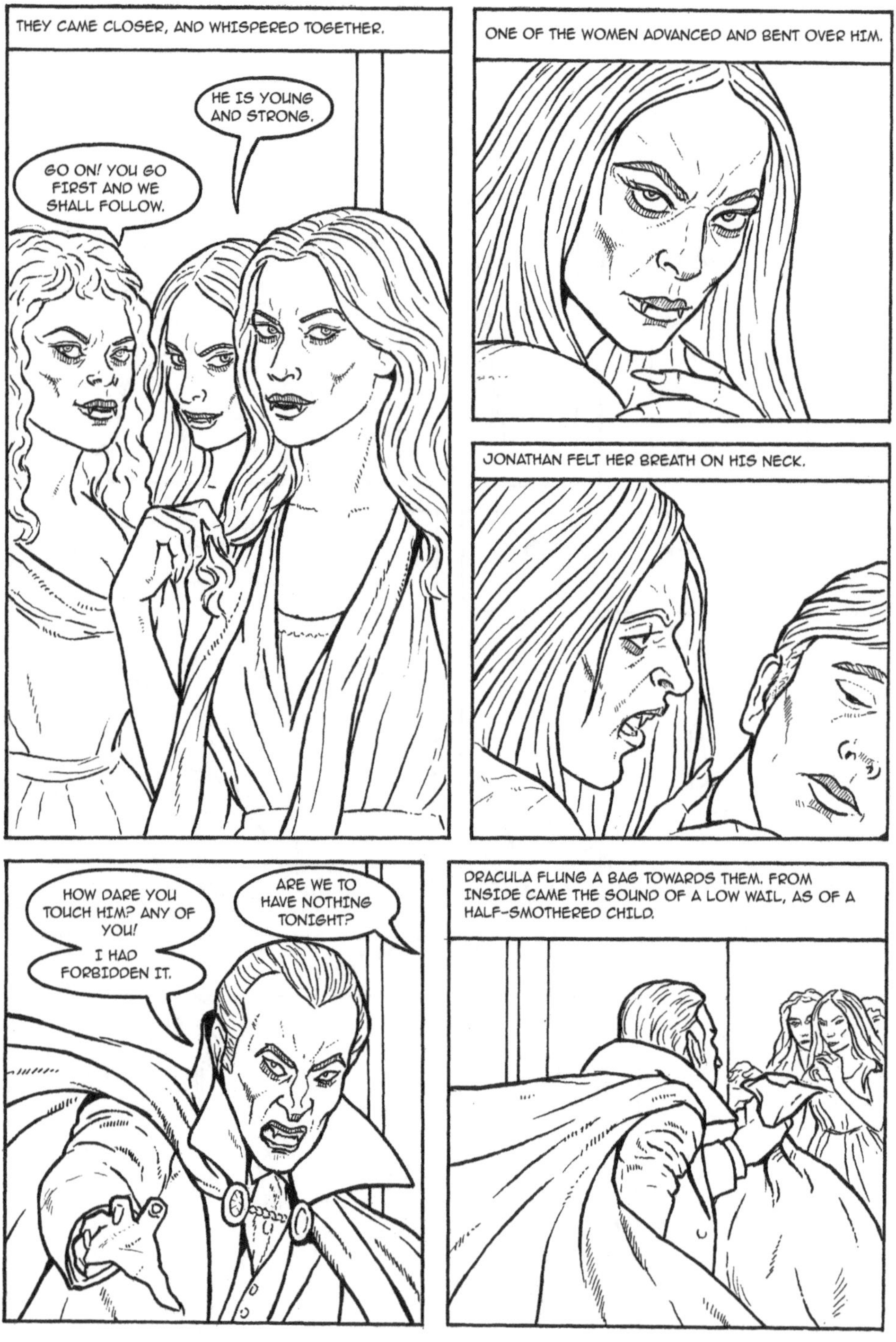

THEY CAME CLOSER, AND WHISPERED TOGETHER.
HE IS YOUNG AND STRONG.
GO ON! YOU GO FIRST AND WE SHALL FOLLOW.
ONE OF THE WOMEN ADVANCED AND BENT OVER HIM.
JONATHAN FELT HER BREATH ON HIS NECK.
HOW DARE YOU TOUCH HIM? ANY OF YOU!
I HAD FORBIDDEN IT.
ARE WE TO HAVE NOTHING TONIGHT?
DRACULA FLUNG A BAG TOWARDS THEM. FROM INSIDE CAME THE SOUND OF A LOW WAIL, AS OF A HALF-SMOTHERED CHILD.

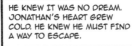
JONATHAN AWOKE IN HIS BEDROOM.

HE KNEW IT WAS NO DREAM. JONATHAN'S HEART GREW COLD. HE KNEW HE MUST FIND A WAY TO ESCAPE.

JONATHAN RAN OUT OF HIS BEDROOM, DOWN THE PASSAGE, DOWN THE GREAT STAIRCASE.

THE GREAT HALL DOOR WAS LOCKED.

HE SEARCHED THE PASSAGE AND FOUND AN UNLOCKED DOOR.

HE FOUND HIMSELF IN A RUINED CHAPEL.

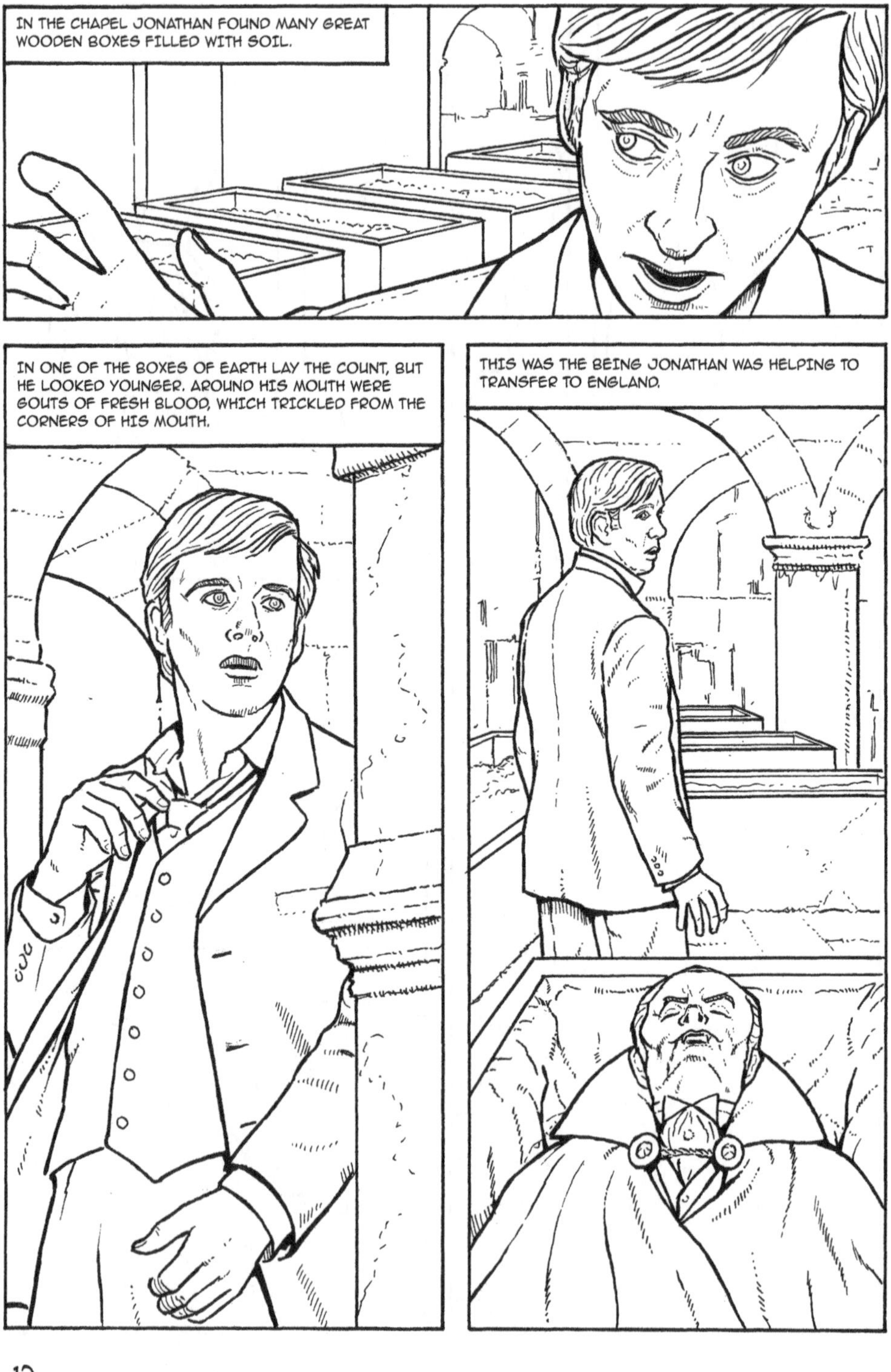
IN THE CHAPEL JONATHAN FOUND MANY GREAT WOODEN BOXES FILLED WITH SOIL.
IN ONE OF THE BOXES OF EARTH LAY THE COUNT, BUT HE LOOKED YOUNGER. AROUND HIS MOUTH WERE GOUTS OF FRESH BLOOD, WHICH TRICKLED FROM THE CORNERS OF HIS MOUTH.
THIS WAS THE BEING JONATHAN WAS HELPING TO TRANSFER TO ENGLAND.

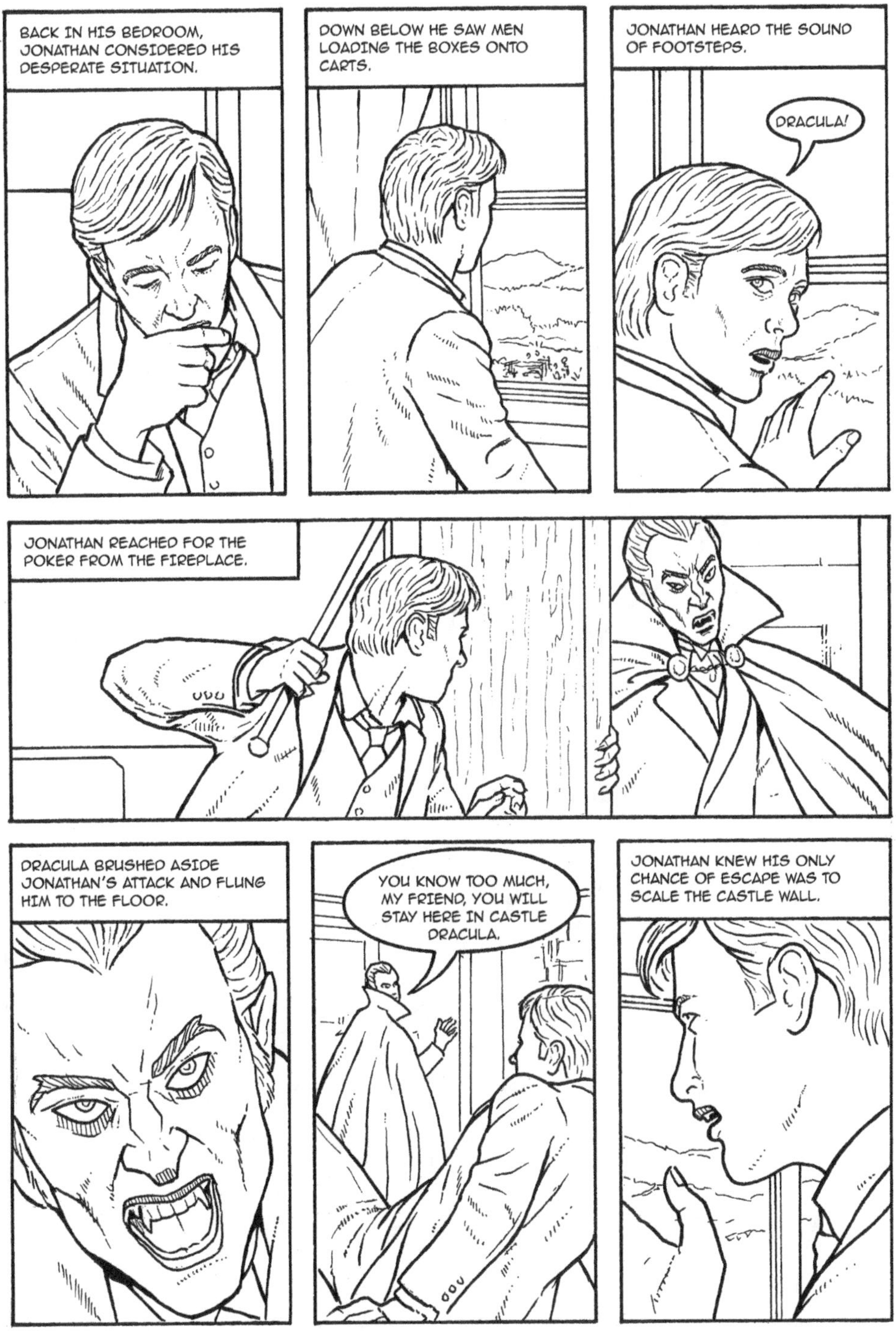
BACK IN HIS BEDROOM, JONATHAN CONSIDERED HIS DESPERATE SITUATION.
DOWN BELOW HE SAW MEN LOADING THE BOXES ONTO CARTS.
JONATHAN HEARD THE SOUND OF FOOTSTEPS.
DRACULA!
JONATHAN REACHED FOR THE POKER FROM THE FIREPLACE.
DRACULA BRUSHED ASIDE JONATHAN'S ATTACK AND FLUNG HIM TO THE FLOOR.
YOU KNOW TOO MUCH, MY FRIEND, YOU WILL STAY HERE IN CASTLE DRACULA.
JONATHAN KNEW HIS ONLY CHANCE OF ESCAPE WAS TO SCALE THE CASTLE WALL.

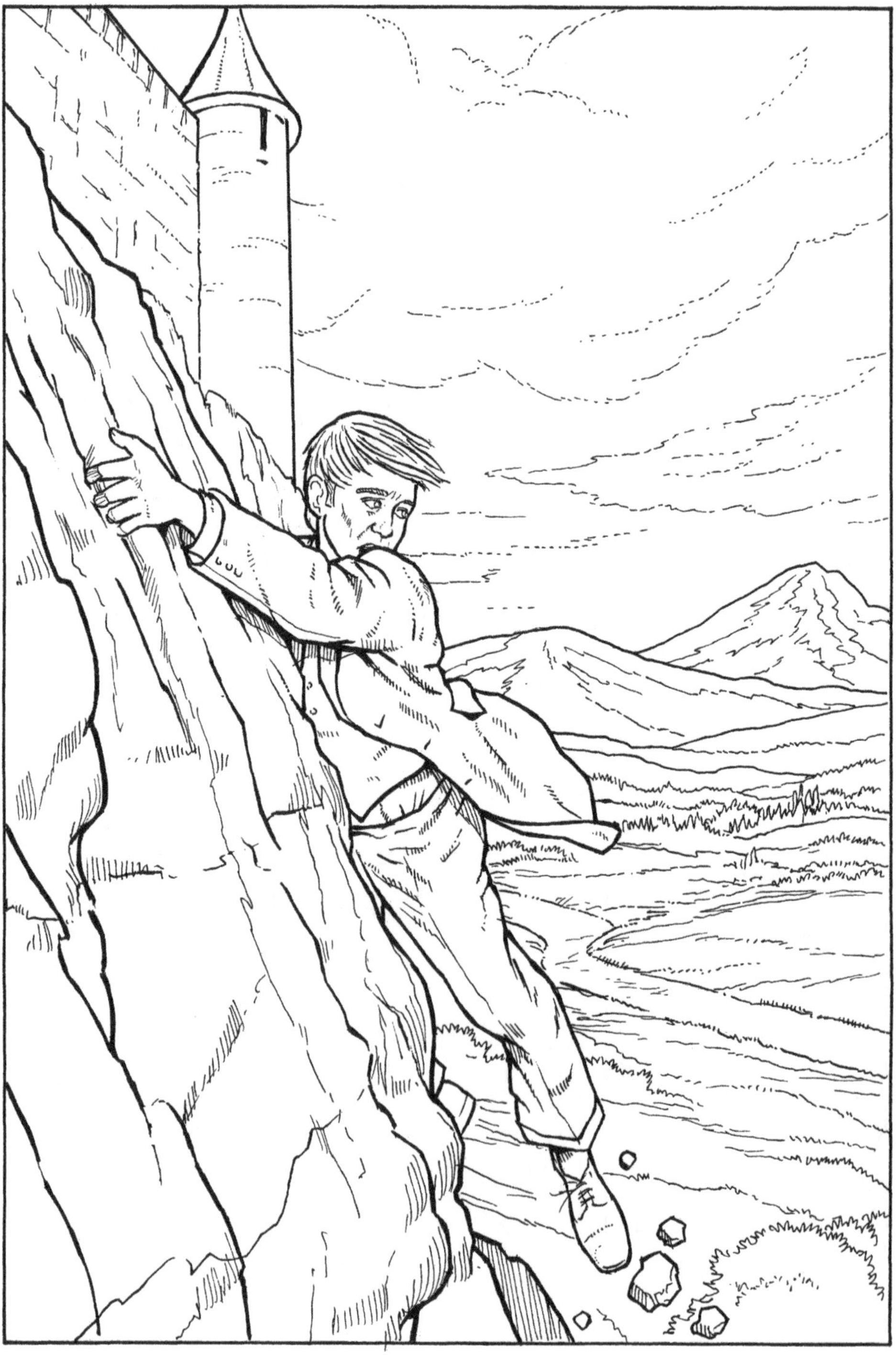

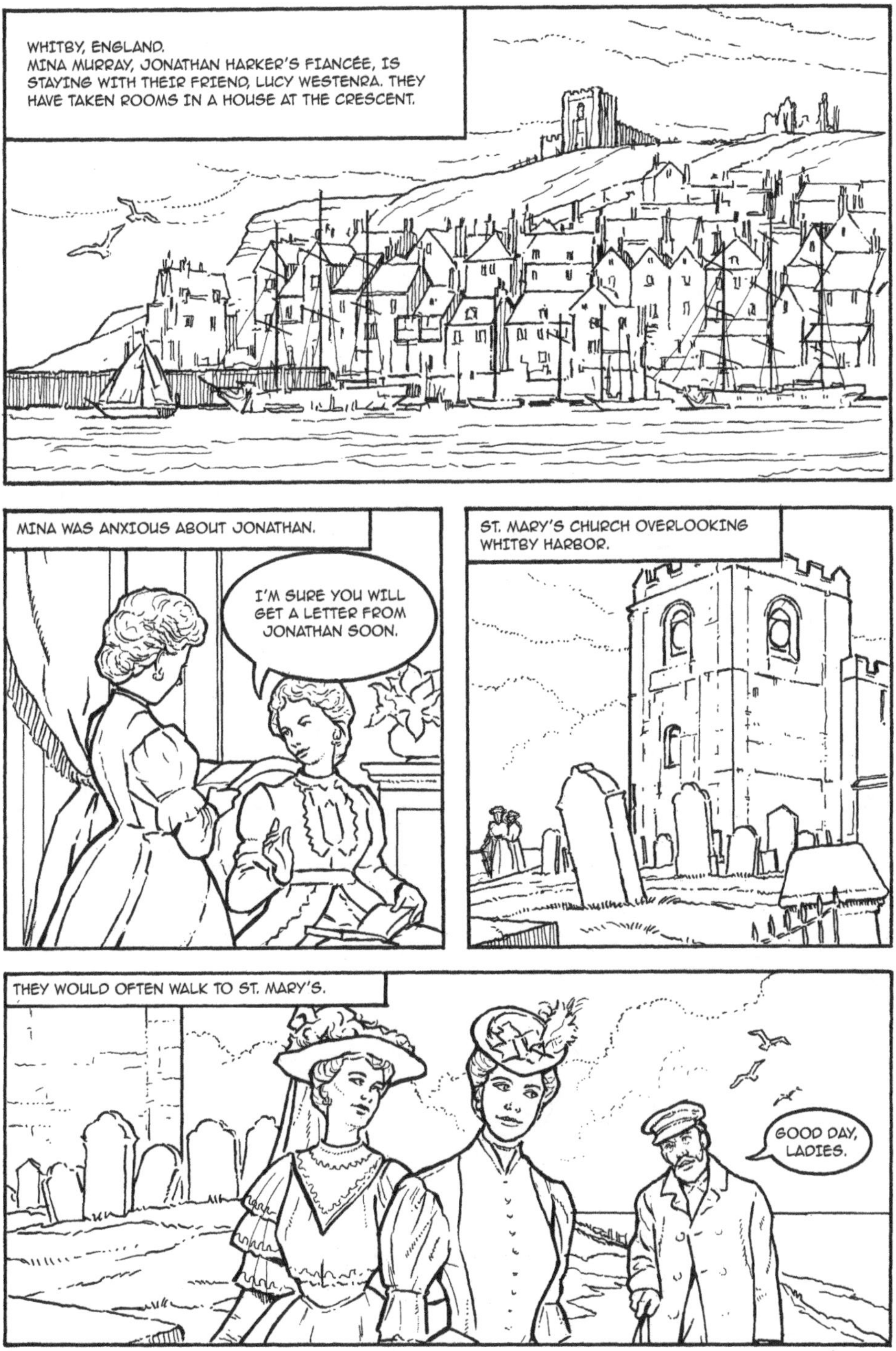
WHITBY, ENGLAND.
MINA MURRAY, JONATHAN HARKER'S FIANCÉE, IS STAYING WITH THEIR FRIEND, LUCY WESTENRA. THEY HAVE TAKEN ROOMS IN A HOUSE AT THE CRESCENT.
MINA WAS ANXIOUS ABOUT JONATHAN.
I'M SURE YOU WILL GET A LETTER FROM JONATHAN SOON.
ST. MARY'S CHURCH OVERLOOKING WHITBY HARBOR.
THEY WOULD OFTEN WALK TO ST. MARY'S.
GOOD DAY, LADIES.

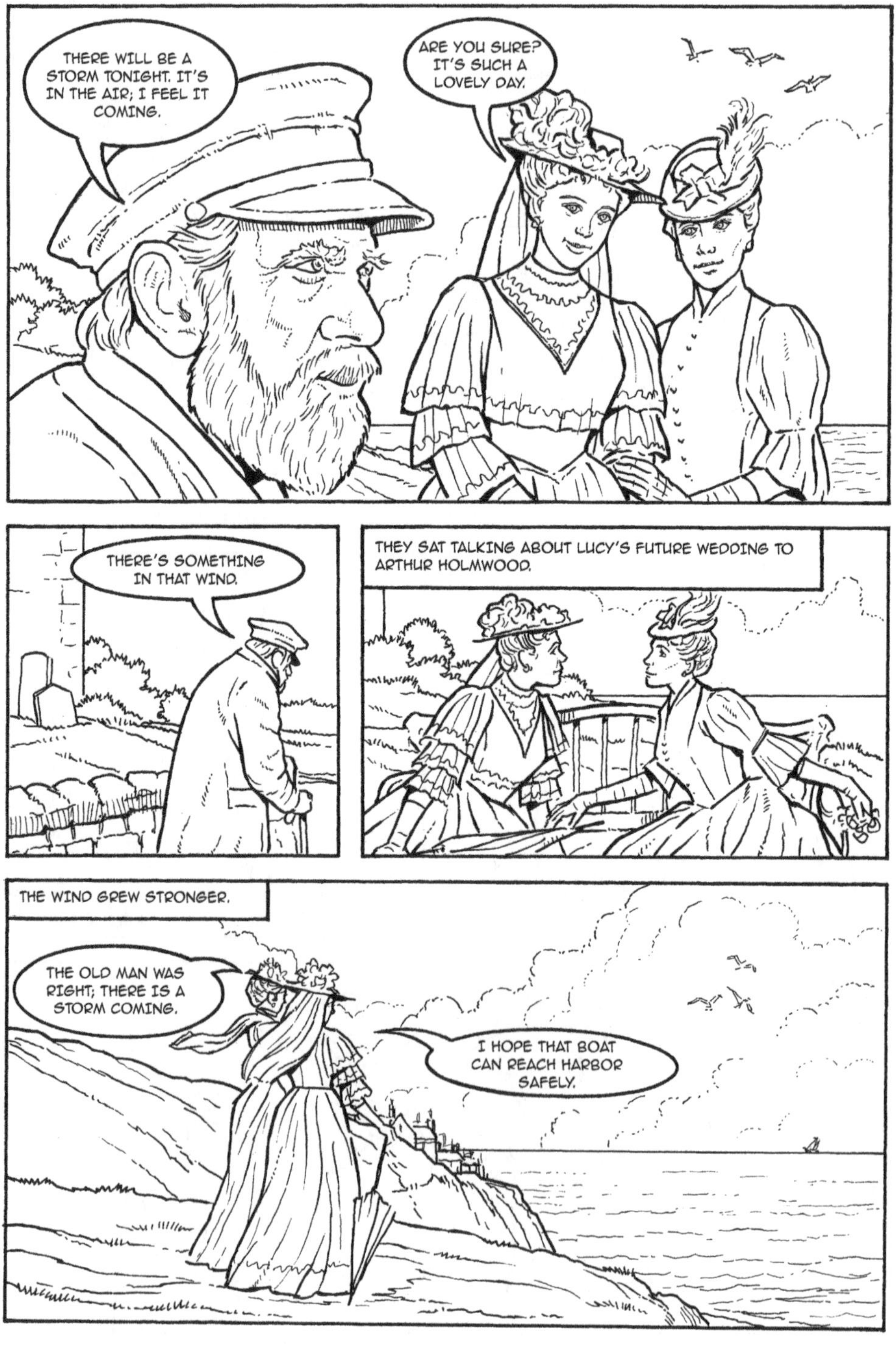
THERE WILL BE A STORM TONIGHT. IT'S IN THE AIR; I FEEL IT COMING.
ARE YOU SURE? IT'S SUCH A LOVELY DAY.
THERE'S SOMETHING IN THAT WIND.
THEY SAT TALKING ABOUT LUCY'S FUTURE WEDDING TO ARTHUR HOLMWOOD.
THE WIND GREW STRONGER.
THE OLD MAN WAS RIGHT; THERE IS A STORM COMING.
I HOPE THAT BOAT CAN REACH HARBOR SAFELY.

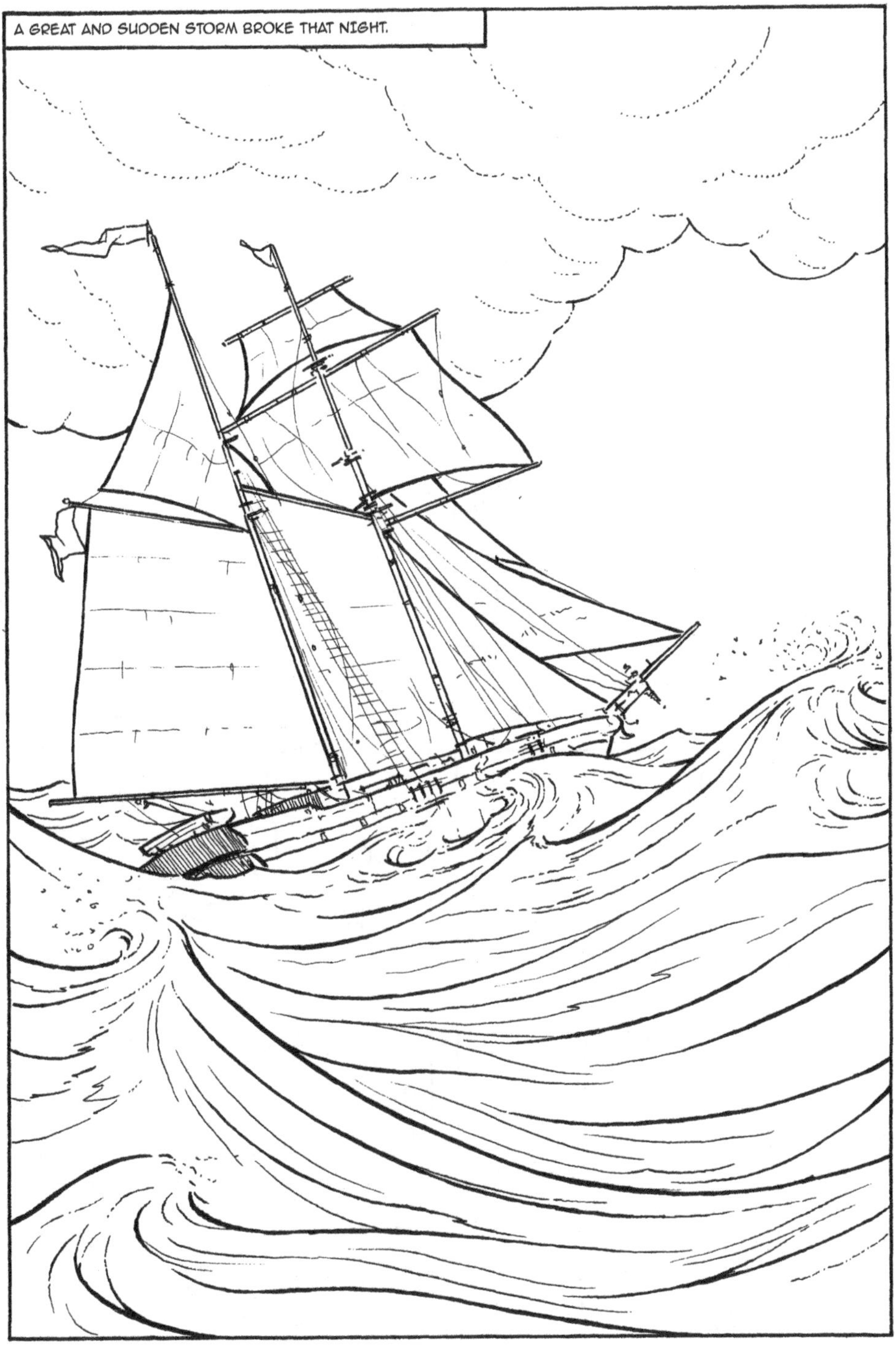
A GREAT AND SUDDEN STORM BROKE THAT NIGHT.

THE BOAT MINA AND LUCY SAW THE EVENING BEFORE CAME TO GROUND UNDER THE CLIFF.

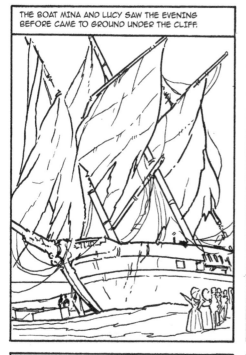

ITS CARGO OF WOODEN BOXES FILLED WITH SOIL WERE STREWN OVER THE BEACH.

A GREAT DOG WAS SEEN LEAPING FROM THE DECK ONTO THE BEACH, MAKING STRAIGHT FOR THE CLIFF.

WHAT DO YOU MAKE OF THAT?

THERE IS SOMETHING VERY ODD ABOUT THIS BOAT.

WE FOUND ONLY ONE BODY ON THE BOAT, THAT OF ITS CAPTAIN.

DEAD FOR SOME DAYS, I WOULD SAY.

TIED TO THE HELM WITH THE CHAIN OF A CRUCIFIX.

THE BOAT WAS A RUSSIAN SCHOONER FROM VARNA CALLED THE *DEMETER*, WITH ONLY A SMALL CARGO. THIS CARGO WAS CONSIGNED TO A WHITBY SOLICITOR OF 7 THE CRESCENT, WHO WENT ONBOARD AND TOOK POSSESSION OF THE BOXES.

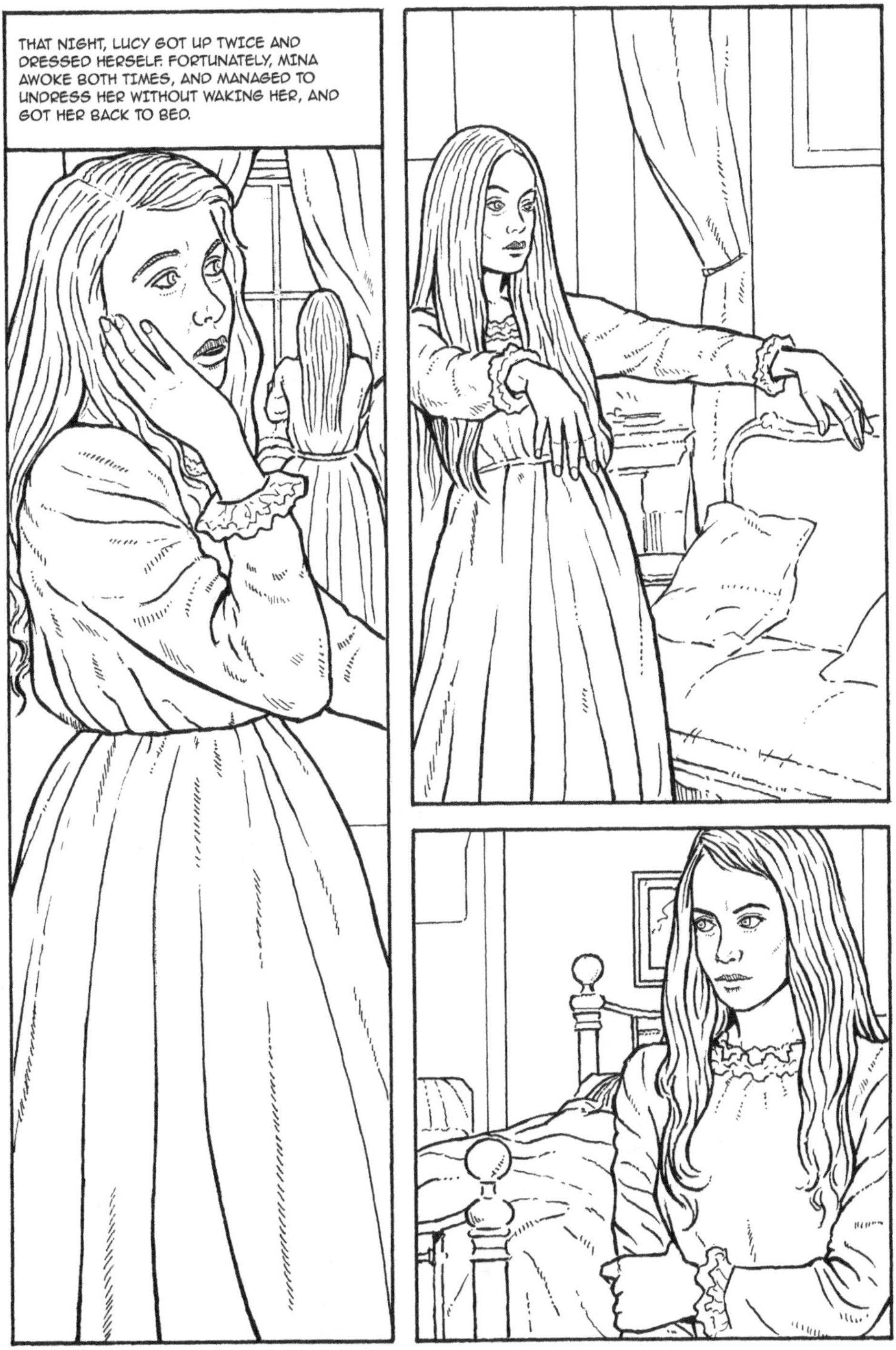
THAT NIGHT, LUCY GOT UP TWICE AND DRESSED HERSELF. FORTUNATELY, MINA AWOKE BOTH TIMES, AND MANAGED TO UNDRESS HER WITHOUT WAKING HER, AND GOT HER BACK TO BED.

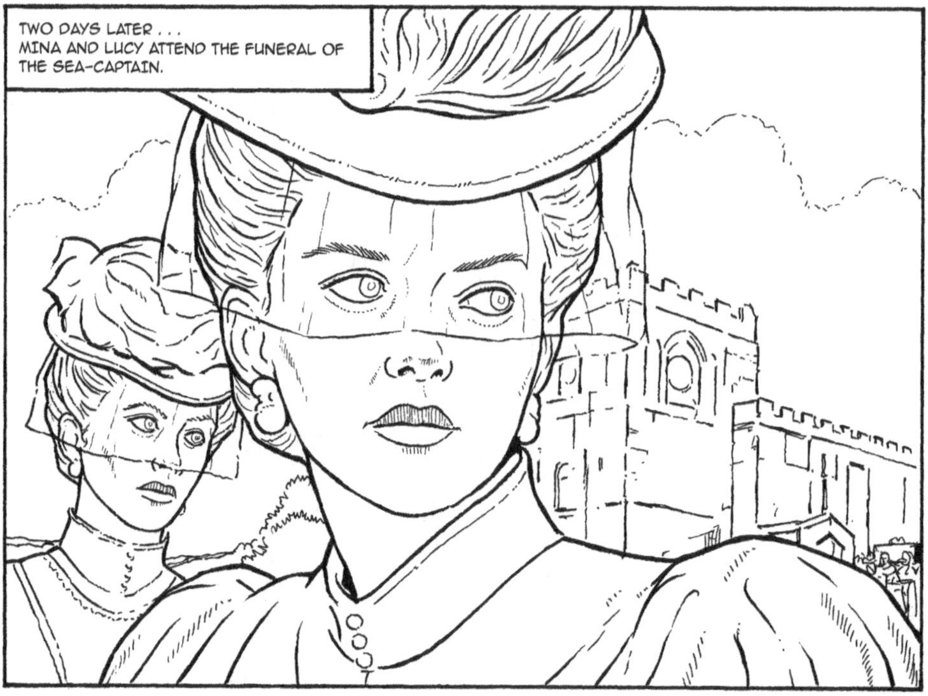
TWO DAYS LATER . . .
MINA AND LUCY ATTEND THE FUNERAL OF THE SEA-CAPTAIN.

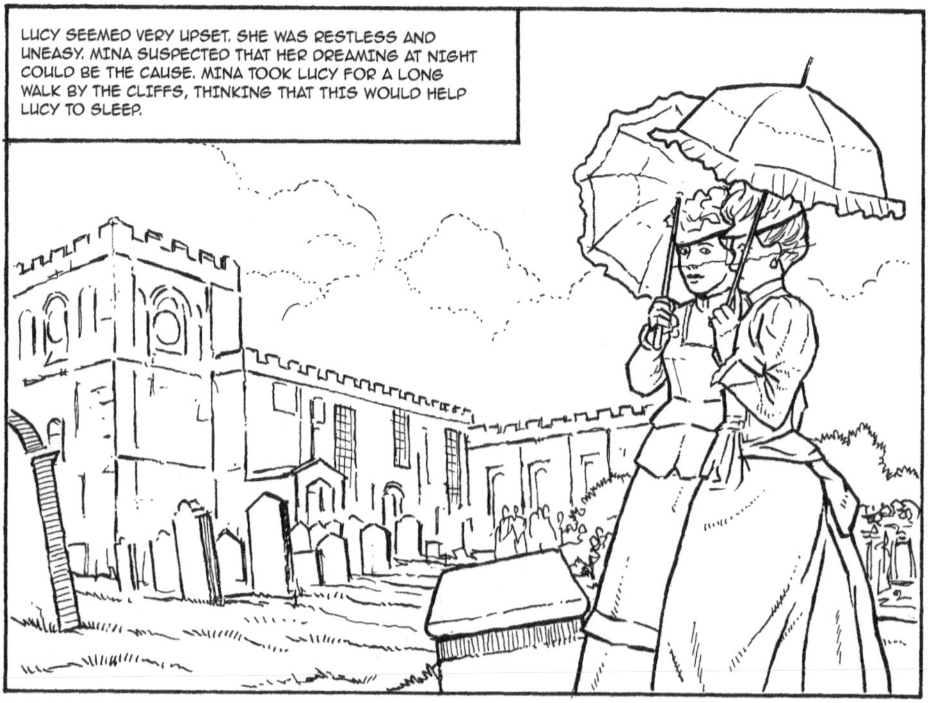
LUCY SEEMED VERY UPSET. SHE WAS RESTLESS AND UNEASY. MINA SUSPECTED THAT HER DREAMING AT NIGHT COULD BE THE CAUSE. MINA TOOK LUCY FOR A LONG WALK BY THE CLIFFS, THINKING THAT THIS WOULD HELP LUCY TO SLEEP.

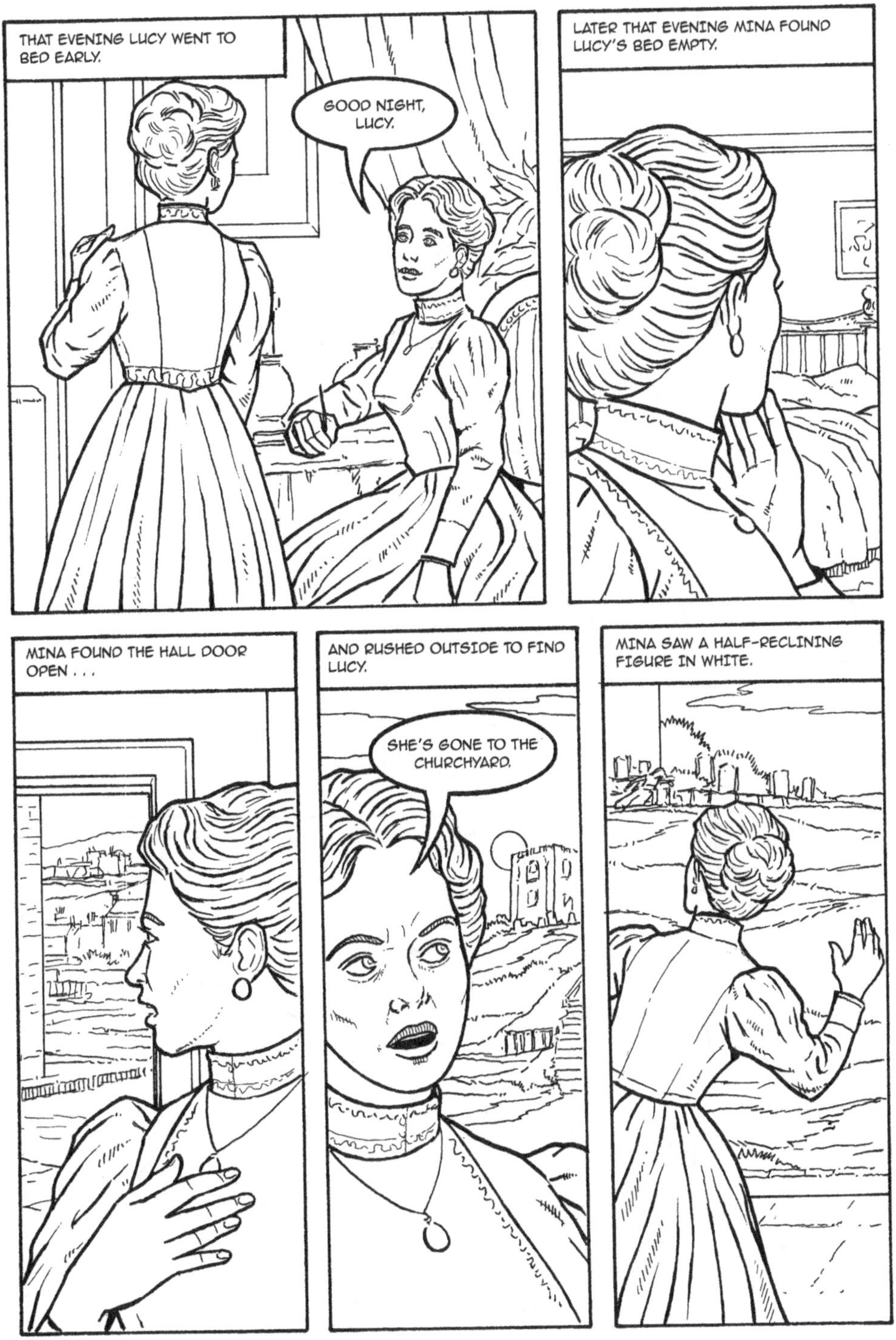
THAT EVENING LUCY WENT TO BED EARLY.
GOOD NIGHT, LUCY.
LATER THAT EVENING MINA FOUND LUCY'S BED EMPTY.
MINA FOUND THE HALL DOOR OPEN . . .
AND RUSHED OUTSIDE TO FIND LUCY.
SHE'S GONE TO THE CHURCHYARD.
MINA SAW A HALF-RECLINING FIGURE IN WHITE.

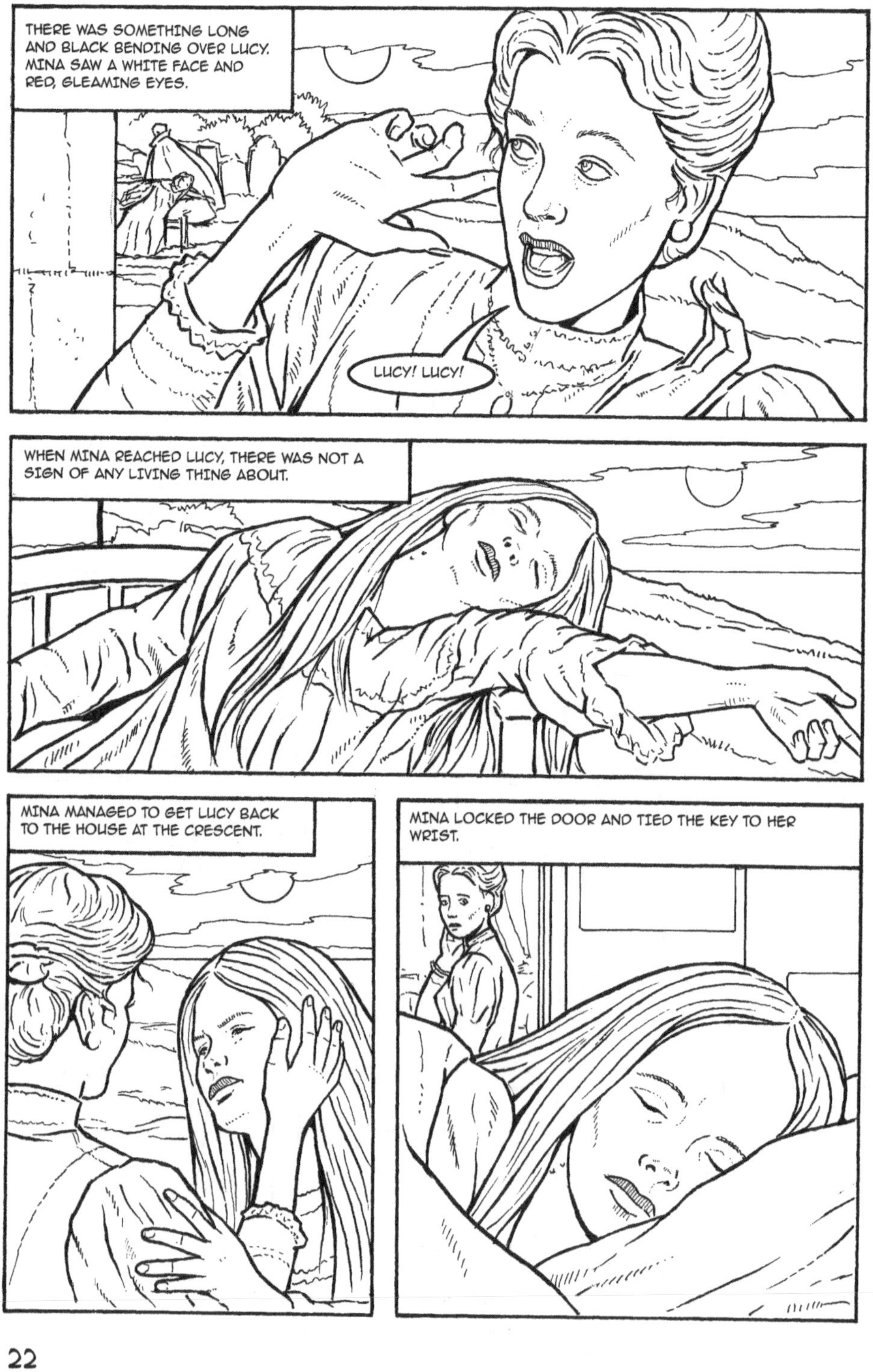
THERE WAS SOMETHING LONG AND BLACK BENDING OVER LUCY. MINA SAW A WHITE FACE AND RED, GLEAMING EYES.
LUCY! LUCY!
WHEN MINA REACHED LUCY, THERE WAS NOT A SIGN OF ANY LIVING THING ABOUT.
MINA MANAGED TO GET LUCY BACK TO THE HOUSE AT THE CRESCENT.
MINA LOCKED THE DOOR AND TIED THE KEY TO HER WRIST.

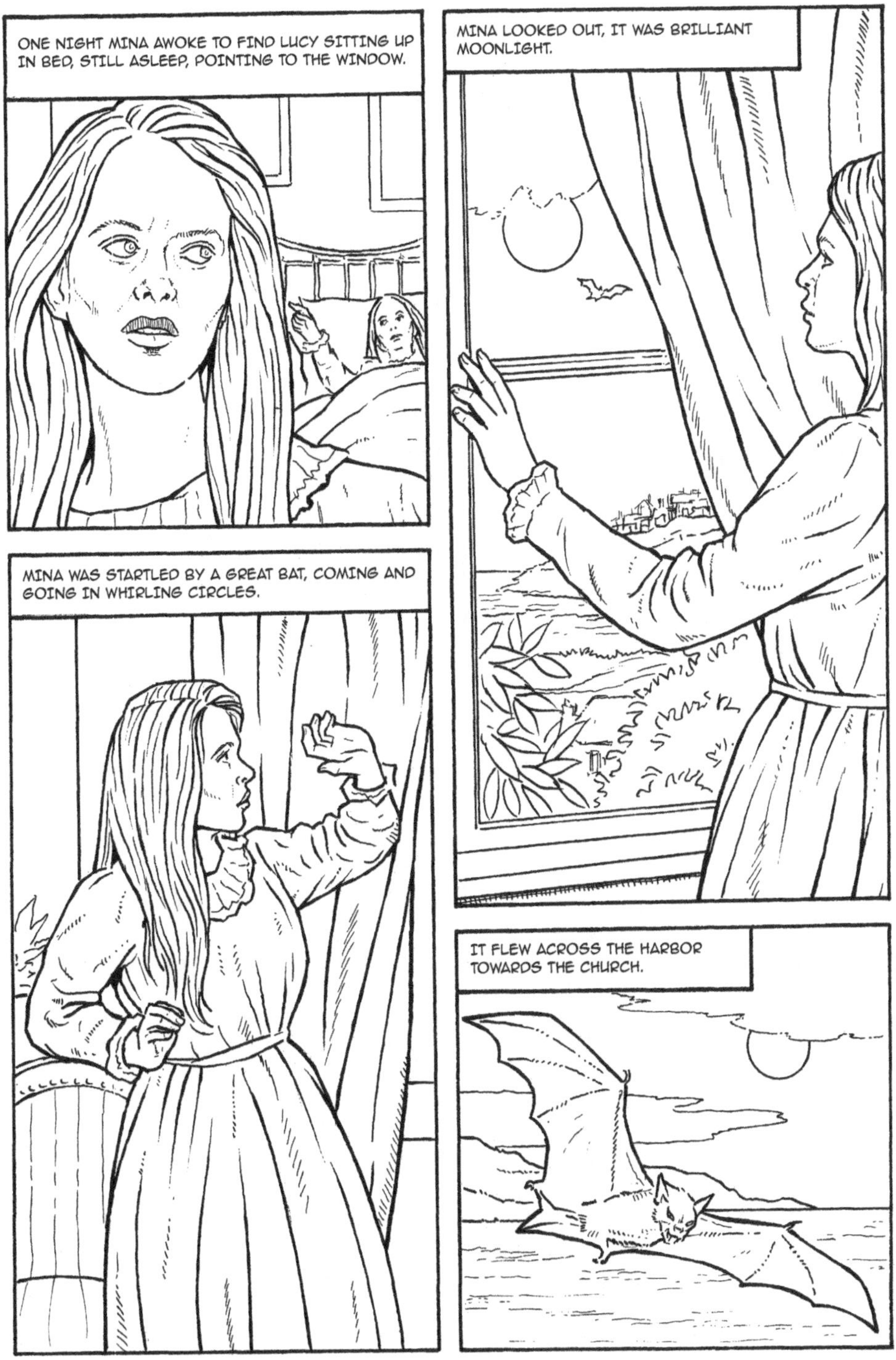
ONE NIGHT MINA AWOKE TO FIND LUCY SITTING UP IN BED, STILL ASLEEP, POINTING TO THE WINDOW.
MINA LOOKED OUT, IT WAS BRILLIANT MOONLIGHT.
MINA WAS STARTLED BY A GREAT BAT, COMING AND GOING IN WHIRLING CIRCLES.
IT FLEW ACROSS THE HARBOR TOWARDS THE CHURCH.

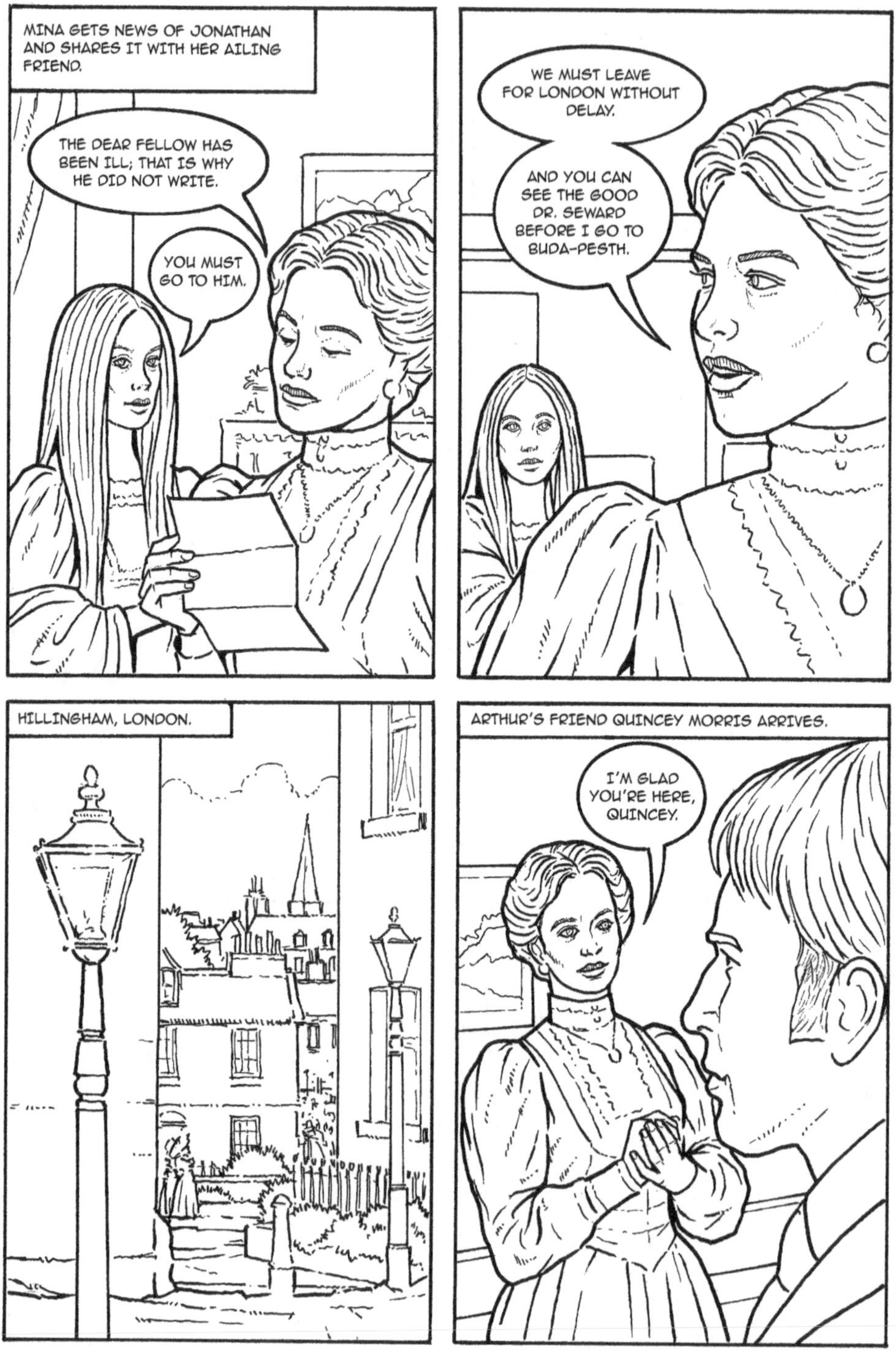
MINA GETS NEWS OF JONATHAN AND SHARES IT WITH HER AILING FRIEND.
THE DEAR FELLOW HAS BEEN ILL; THAT IS WHY HE DID NOT WRITE.
YOU MUST GO TO HIM.
WE MUST LEAVE FOR LONDON WITHOUT DELAY.
AND YOU CAN SEE THE GOOD DR. SEWARD BEFORE I GO TO BUDA-PESTH.
HILLINGHAM, LONDON.
ARTHUR'S FRIEND QUINCEY MORRIS ARRIVES.
I'M GLAD YOU'RE HERE, QUINCEY.

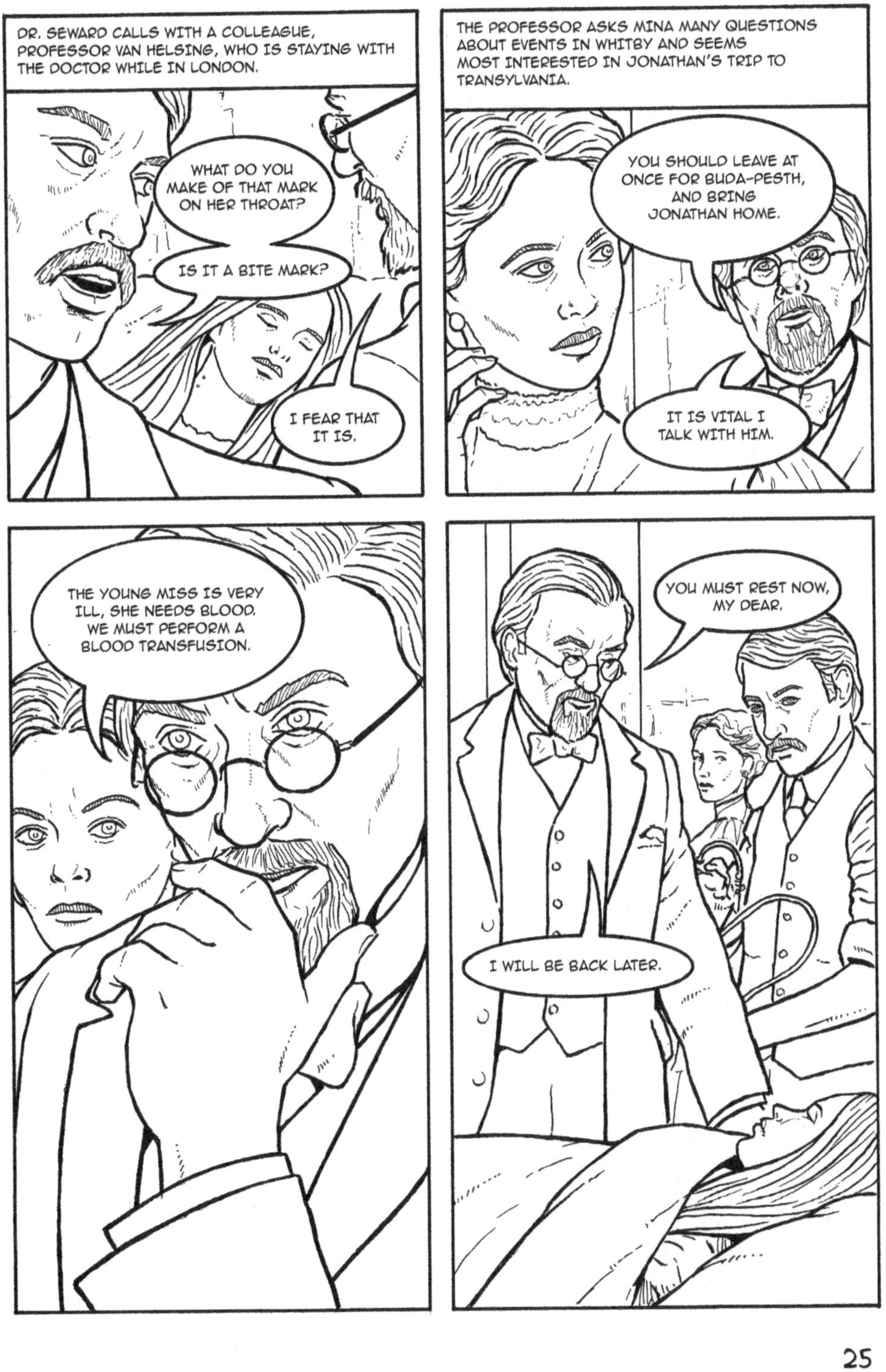

DR. SEWARD CALLS WITH A COLLEAGUE, PROFESSOR VAN HELSING, WHO IS STAYING WITH THE DOCTOR WHILE IN LONDON.
WHAT DO YOU MAKE OF THAT MARK ON HER THROAT?
IS IT A BITE MARK?
I FEAR THAT IT IS.
THE PROFESSOR ASKS MINA MANY QUESTIONS ABOUT EVENTS IN WHITBY AND SEEMS MOST INTERESTED IN JONATHAN'S TRIP TO TRANSYLVANIA.
YOU SHOULD LEAVE AT ONCE FOR BUDA-PESTH, AND BRING JONATHAN HOME.
IT IS VITAL I TALK WITH HIM.
THE YOUNG MISS IS VERY ILL, SHE NEEDS BLOOD. WE MUST PERFORM A BLOOD TRANSFUSION.
YOU MUST REST NOW, MY DEAR.
I WILL BE BACK LATER.

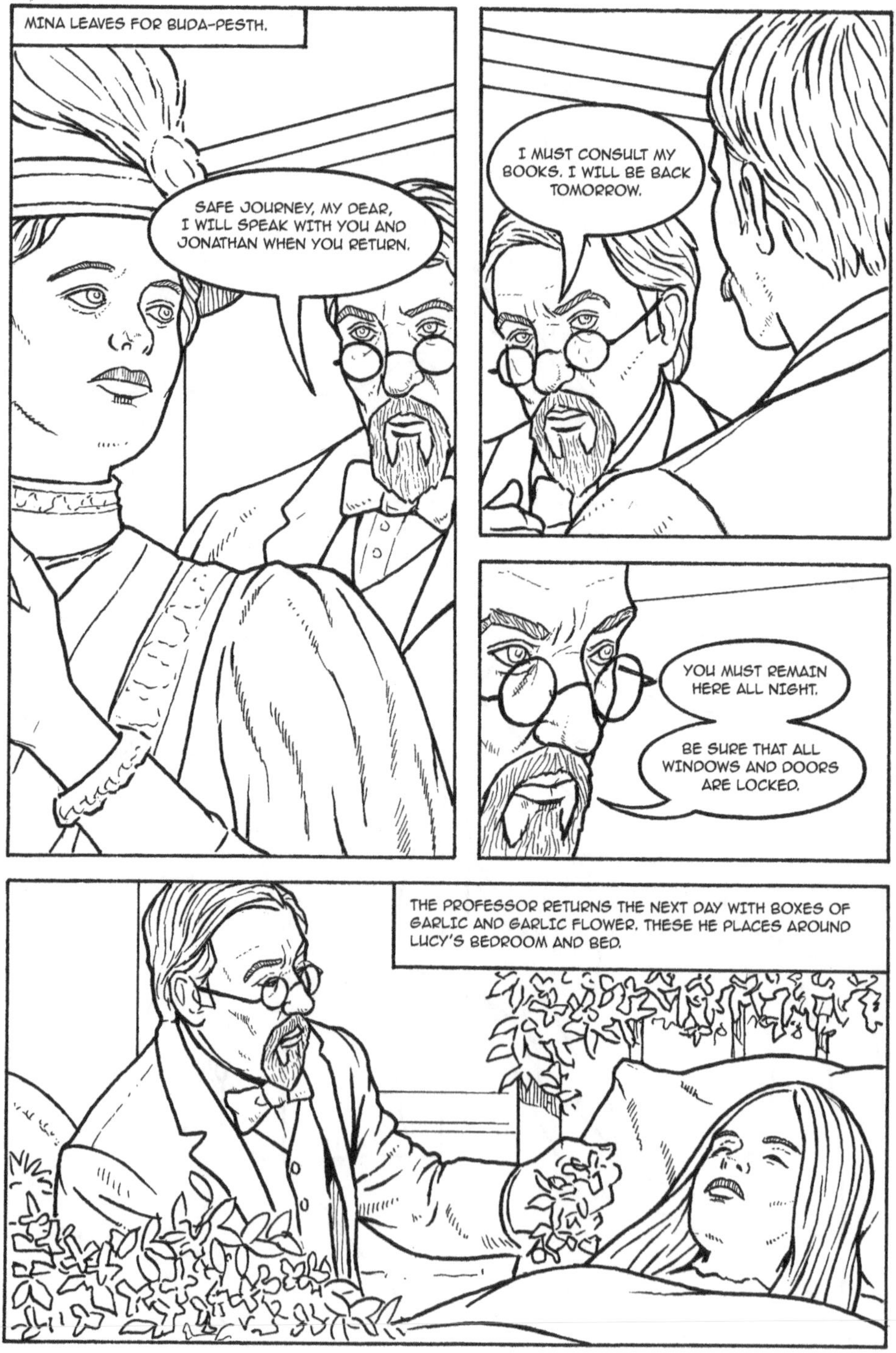
MINA LEAVES FOR BUDA-PESTH.
SAFE JOURNEY, MY DEAR, I WILL SPEAK WITH YOU AND JONATHAN WHEN YOU RETURN.
I MUST CONSULT MY BOOKS. I WILL BE BACK TOMORROW.
YOU MUST REMAIN HERE ALL NIGHT.
BE SURE THAT ALL WINDOWS AND DOORS ARE LOCKED.
THE PROFESSOR RETURNS THE NEXT DAY WITH BOXES OF GARLIC AND GARLIC FLOWER. THESE HE PLACES AROUND LUCY'S BEDROOM AND BED.

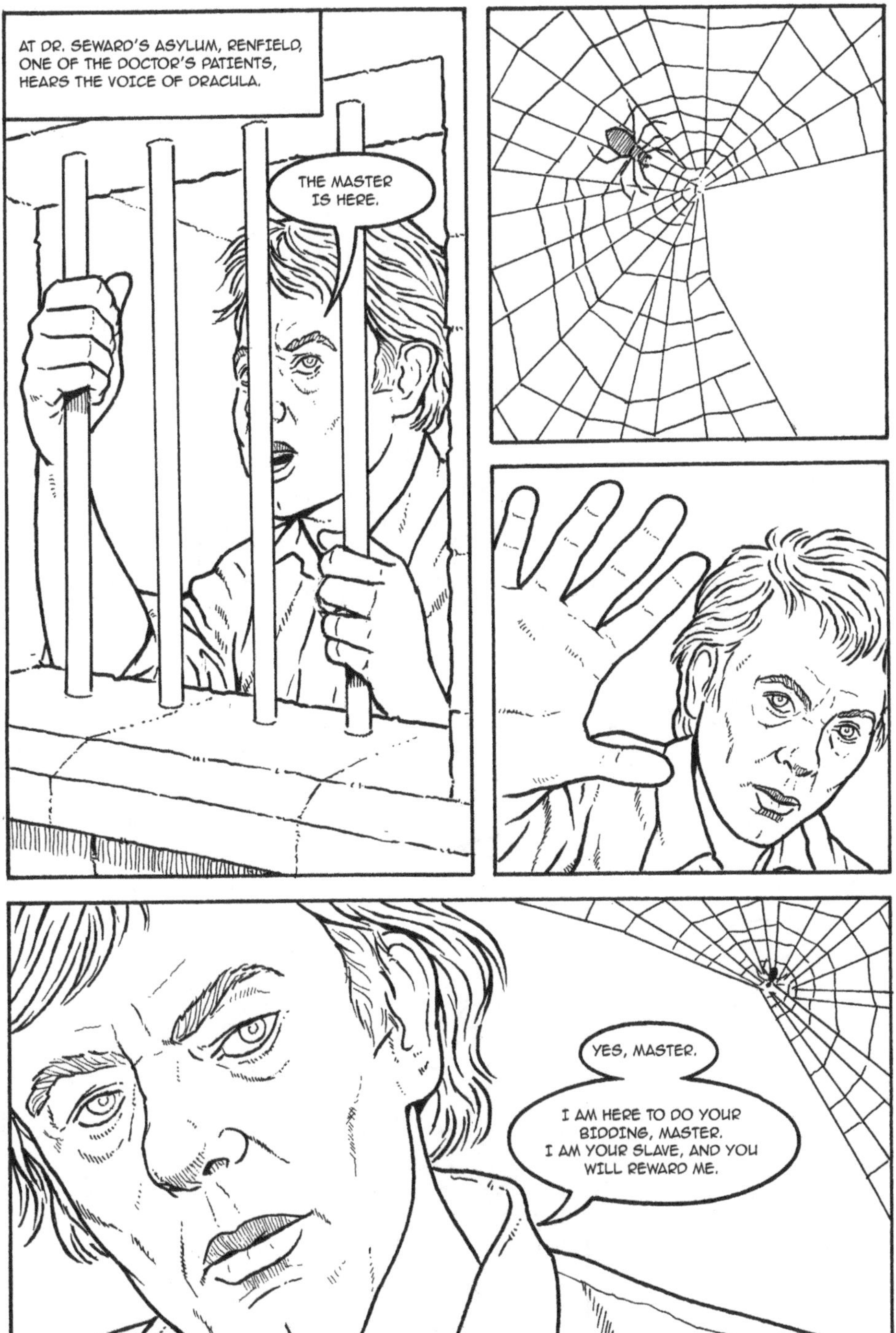
AT DR. SEWARD'S ASYLUM, RENFIELD, ONE OF THE DOCTOR'S PATIENTS, HEARS THE VOICE OF DRACULA.
THE MASTER IS HERE.
YES, MASTER.
I AM HERE TO DO YOUR BIDDING, MASTER. I AM YOUR SLAVE, AND YOU WILL REWARD ME.

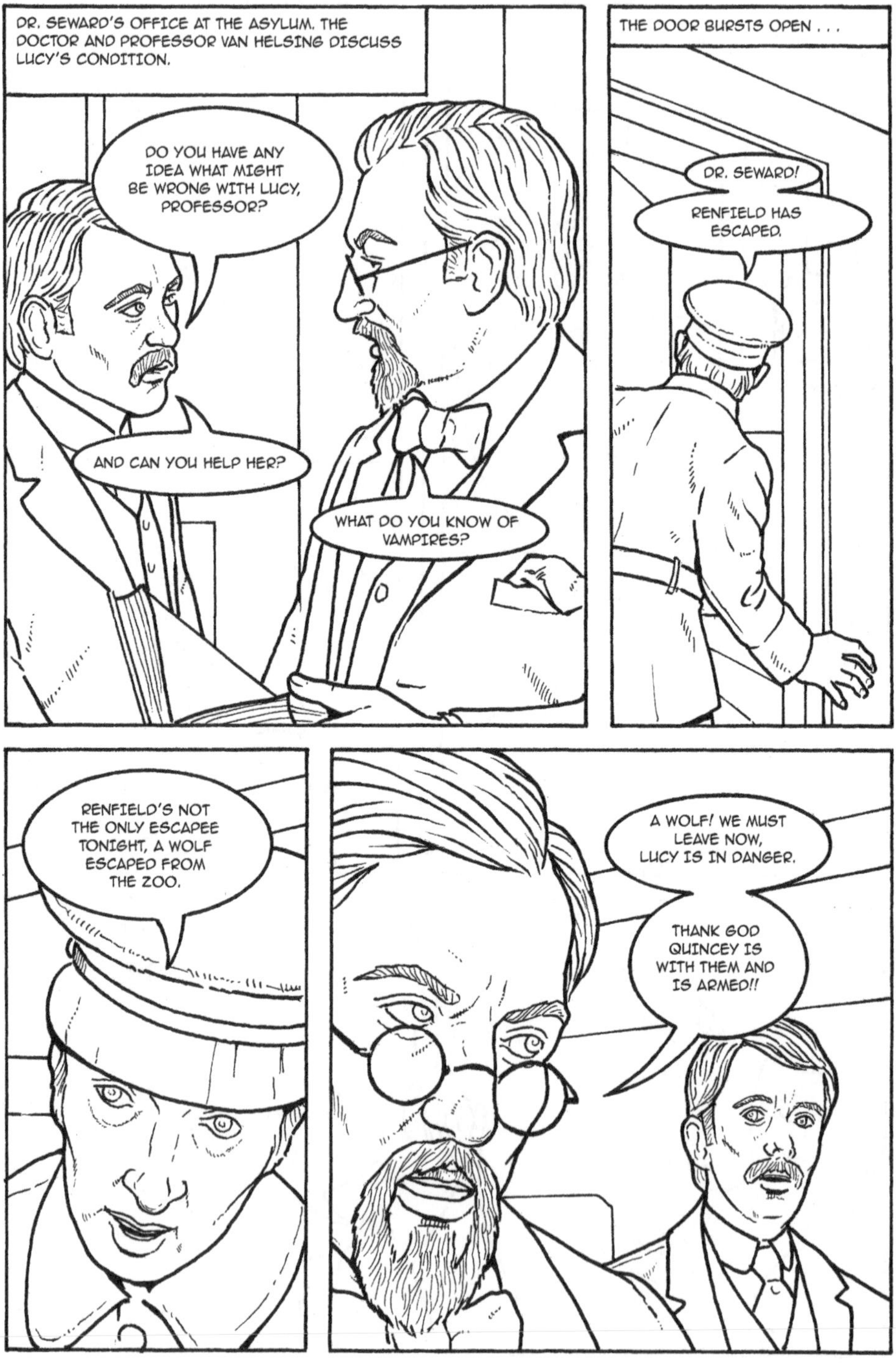
DR. SEWARD'S OFFICE AT THE ASYLUM. THE DOCTOR AND PROFESSOR VAN HELSING DISCUSS LUCY'S CONDITION.
DO YOU HAVE ANY IDEA WHAT MIGHT BE WRONG WITH LUCY, PROFESSOR?
AND CAN YOU HELP HER?
WHAT DO YOU KNOW OF VAMPIRES?
THE DOOR BURSTS OPEN . . .
DR. SEWARD!
RENFIELD HAS ESCAPED.
RENFIELD'S NOT THE ONLY ESCAPEE TONIGHT, A WOLF ESCAPED FROM THE ZOO.
A WOLF! WE MUST LEAVE NOW, LUCY IS IN DANGER.
THANK GOD QUINCEY IS WITH THEM AND IS ARMED!!

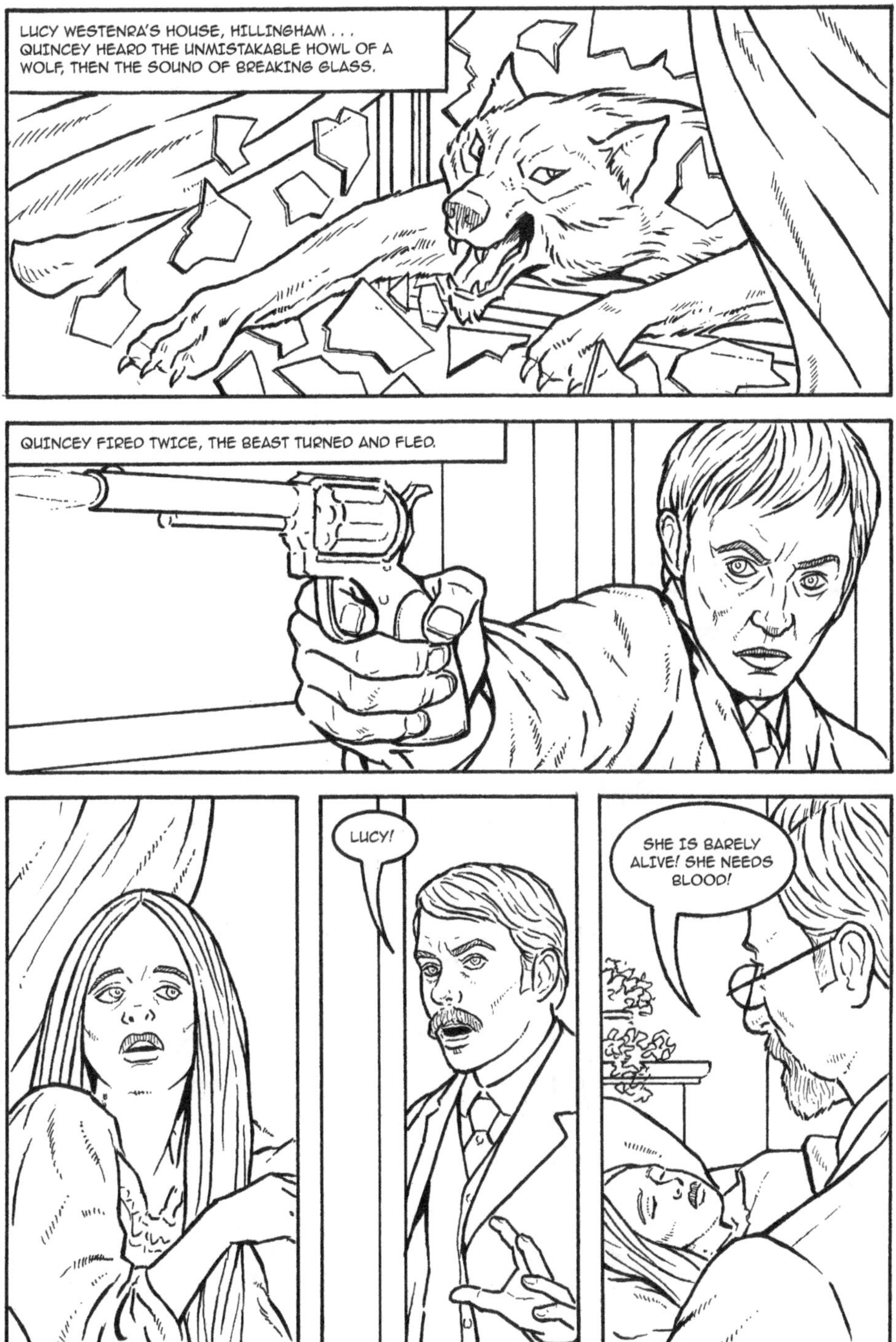
LUCY WESTENRA'S HOUSE, HILLINGHAM . . .
QUINCEY HEARD THE UNMISTAKABLE HOWL OF A WOLF, THEN THE SOUND OF BREAKING GLASS.
QUINCEY FIRED TWICE, THE BEAST TURNED AND FLED.
LUCY!
SHE IS BARELY ALIVE! SHE NEEDS BLOOD!

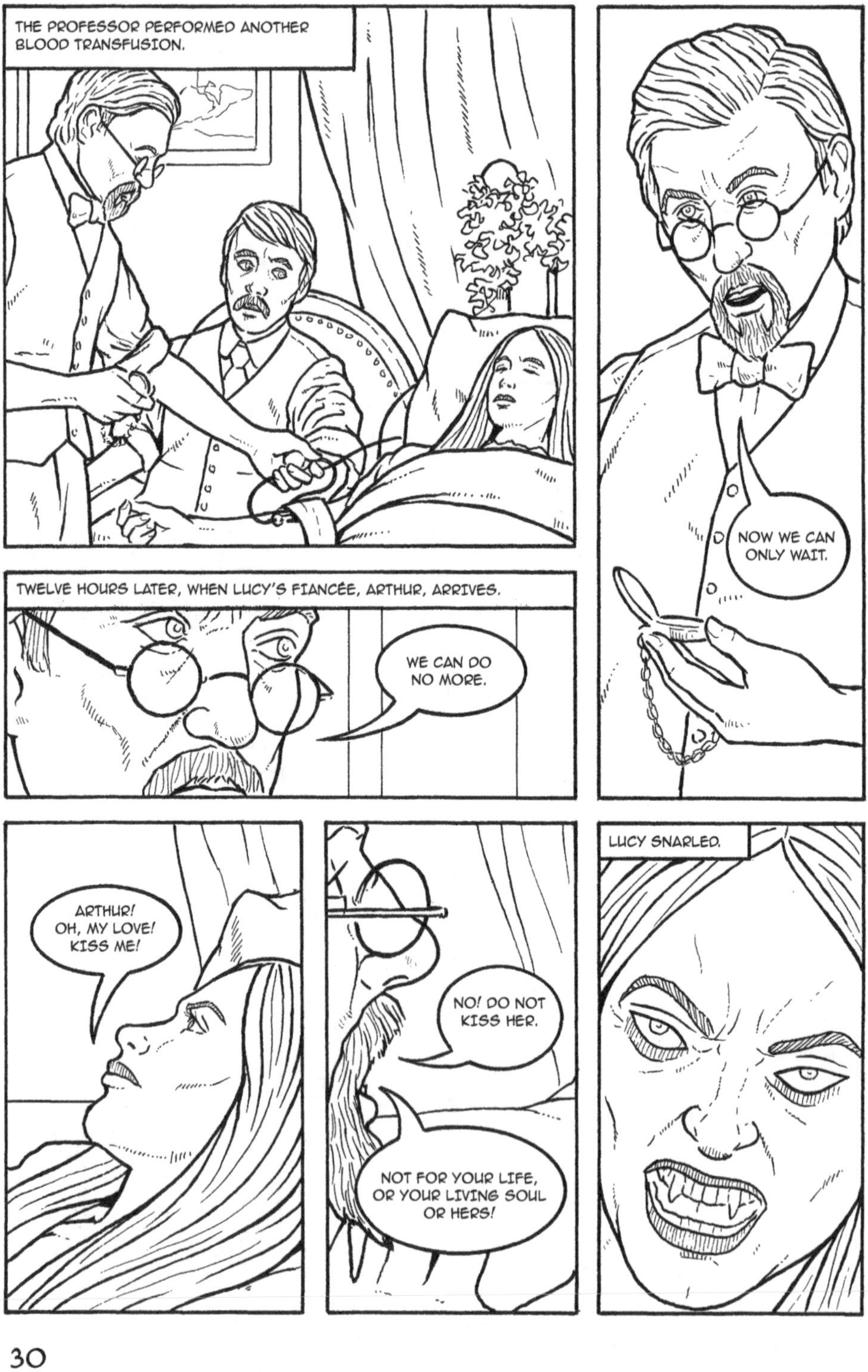
THE PROFESSOR PERFORMED ANOTHER BLOOD TRANSFUSION.
NOW WE CAN ONLY WAIT.
TWELVE HOURS LATER, WHEN LUCY'S FIANCÉE, ARTHUR, ARRIVES.
WE CAN DO NO MORE.
ARTHUR! OH, MY LOVE! KISS ME!
NO! DO NOT KISS HER.
NOT FOR YOUR LIFE, OR YOUR LIVING SOUL OR HERS!
LUCY SNARLED.

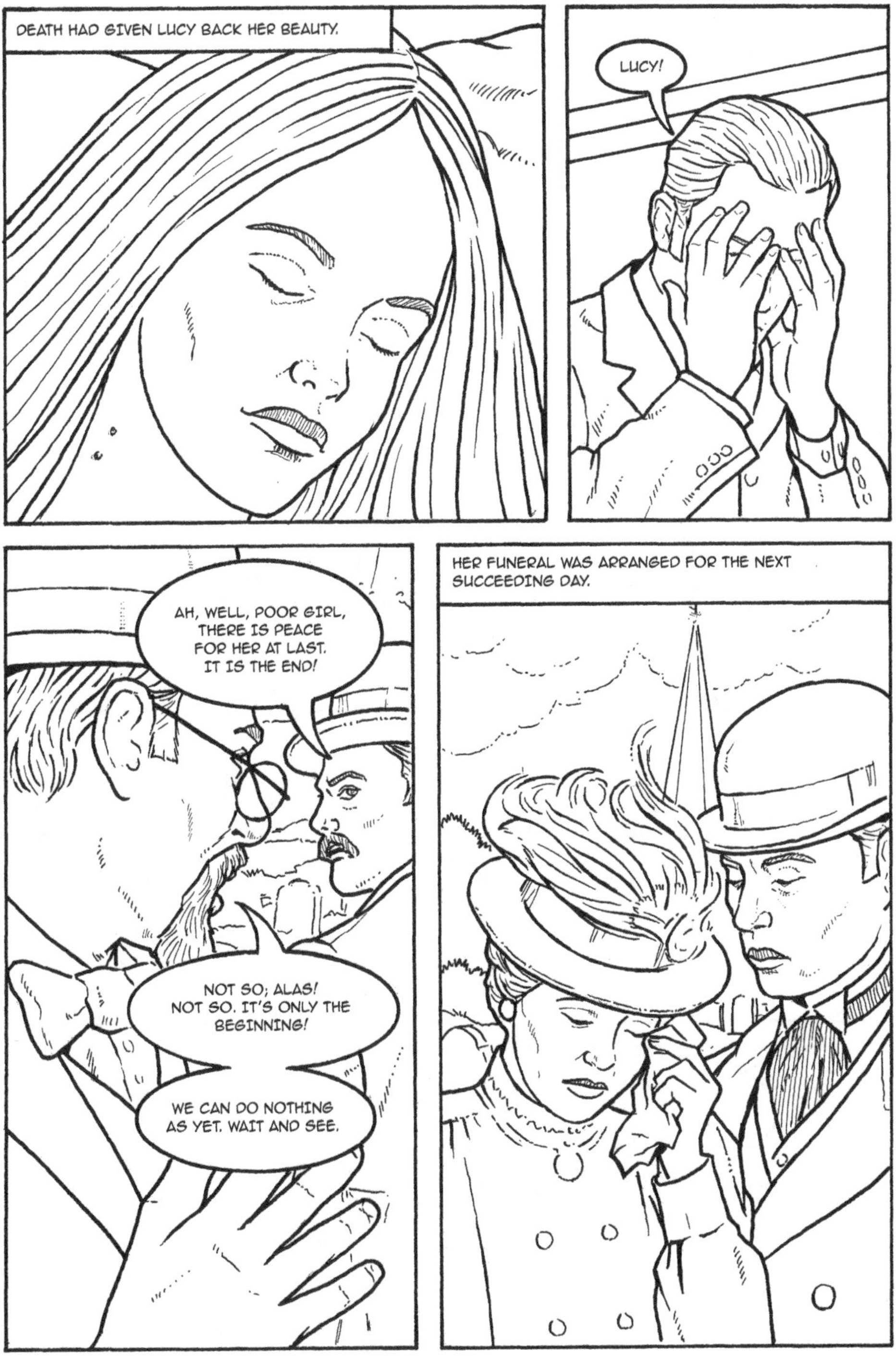
DEATH HAD GIVEN LUCY BACK HER BEAUTY.
LUCY!
AH, WELL, POOR GIRL, THERE IS PEACE FOR HER AT LAST. IT IS THE END!
NOT SO; ALAS! NOT SO. IT'S ONLY THE BEGINNING!
WE CAN DO NOTHING AS YET. WAIT AND SEE.
HER FUNERAL WAS ARRANGED FOR THE NEXT SUCCEEDING DAY.

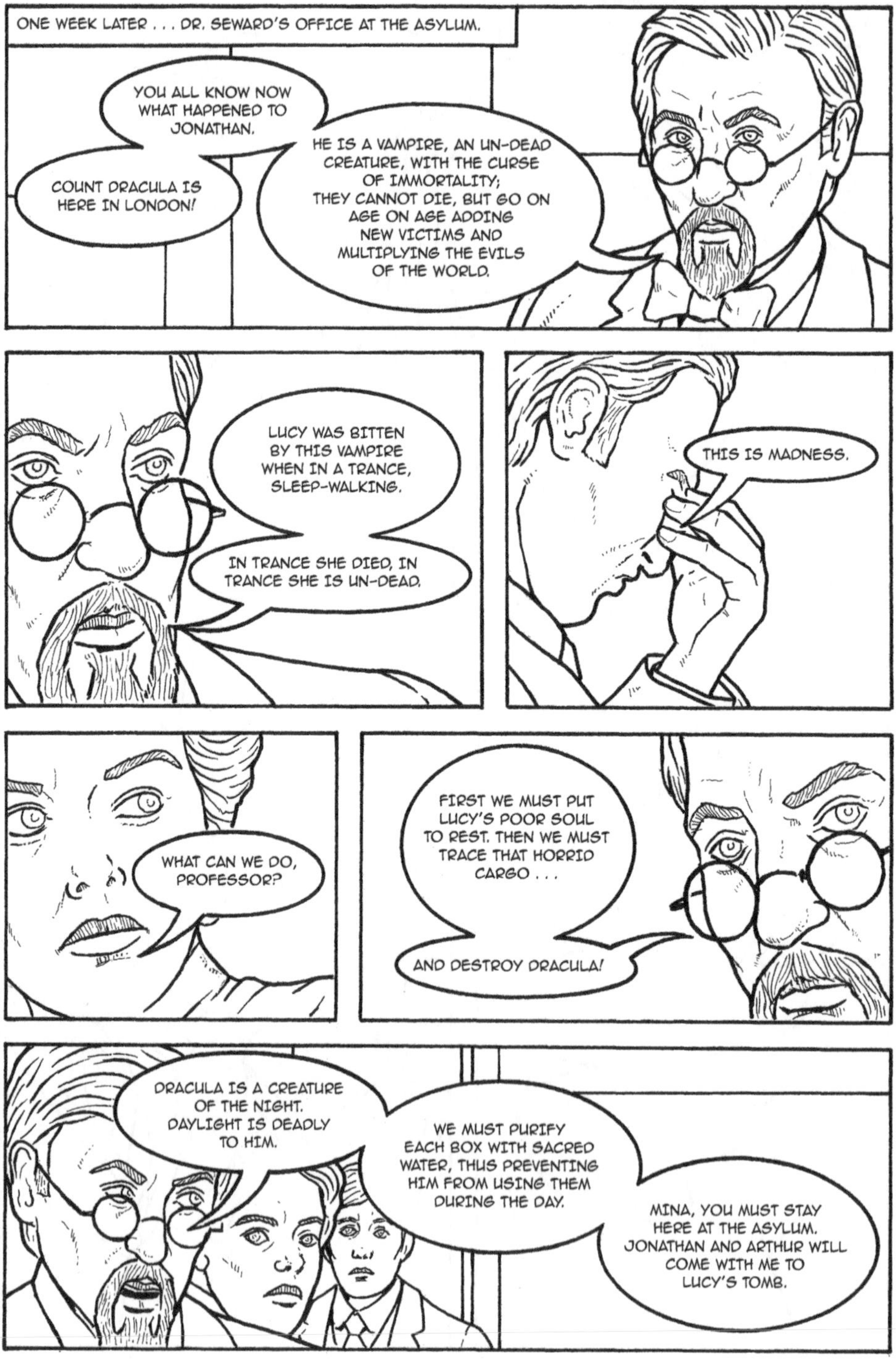
ONE WEEK LATER . . . DR. SEWARD'S OFFICE AT THE ASYLUM.
YOU ALL KNOW NOW WHAT HAPPENED TO JONATHAN.
COUNT DRACULA IS HERE IN LONDON!
HE IS A VAMPIRE, AN UN-DEAD CREATURE, WITH THE CURSE OF IMMORTALITY; THEY CANNOT DIE, BUT GO ON AGE ON AGE ADDING NEW VICTIMS AND MULTIPLYING THE EVILS OF THE WORLD.
LUCY WAS BITTEN BY THIS VAMPIRE WHEN IN A TRANCE, SLEEP-WALKING.
IN TRANCE SHE DIED, IN TRANCE SHE IS UN-DEAD.
THIS IS MADNESS.
WHAT CAN WE DO, PROFESSOR?
FIRST WE MUST PUT LUCY'S POOR SOUL TO REST. THEN WE MUST TRACE THAT HORRID CARGO . . .
AND DESTROY DRACULA!
DRACULA IS A CREATURE OF THE NIGHT. DAYLIGHT IS DEADLY TO HIM.
WE MUST PURIFY EACH BOX WITH SACRED WATER, THUS PREVENTING HIM FROM USING THEM DURING THE DAY.
MINA, YOU MUST STAY HERE AT THE ASYLUM. JONATHAN AND ARTHUR WILL COME WITH ME TO LUCY'S TOMB.

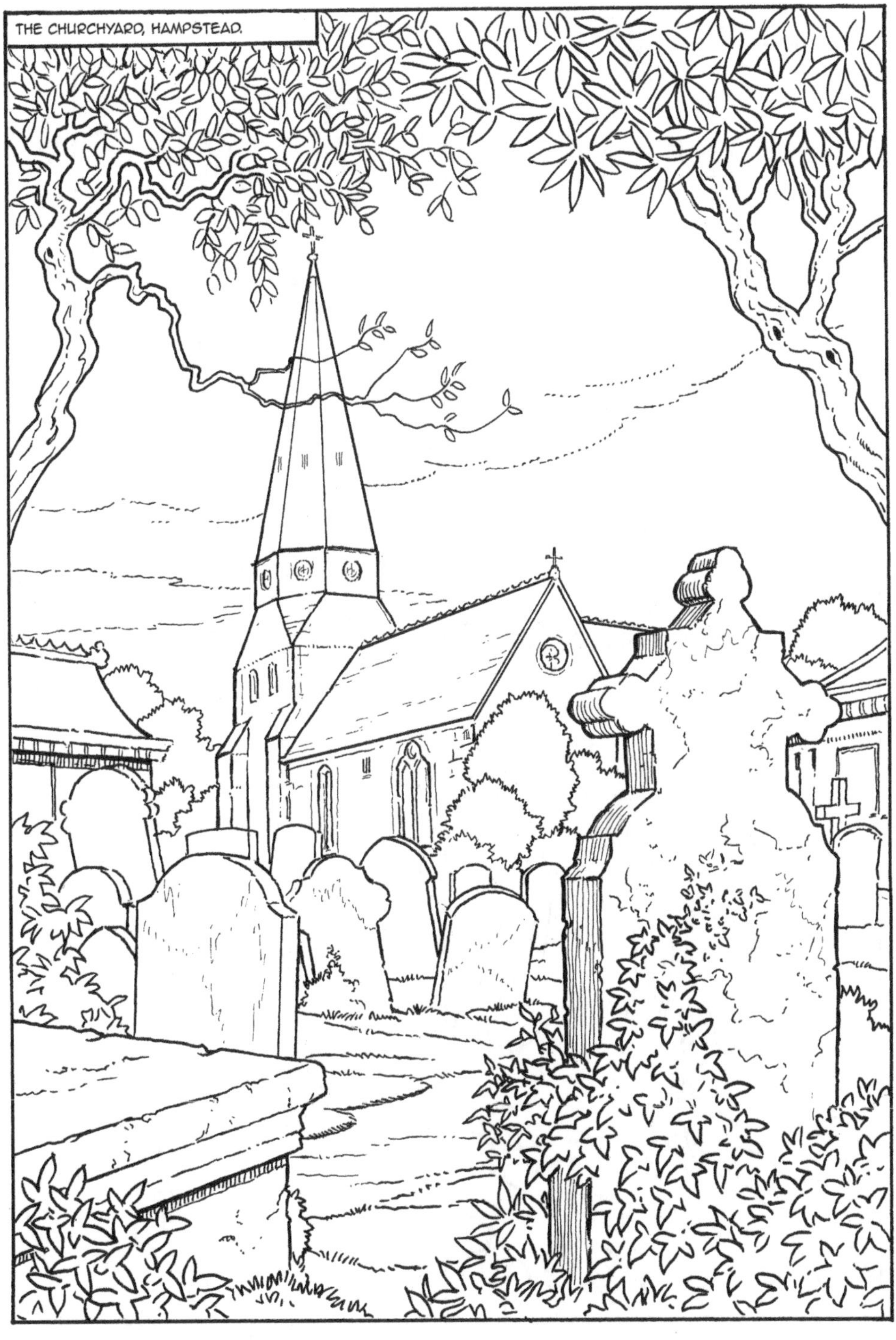
THE CHURCHYARD, HAMPSTEAD.

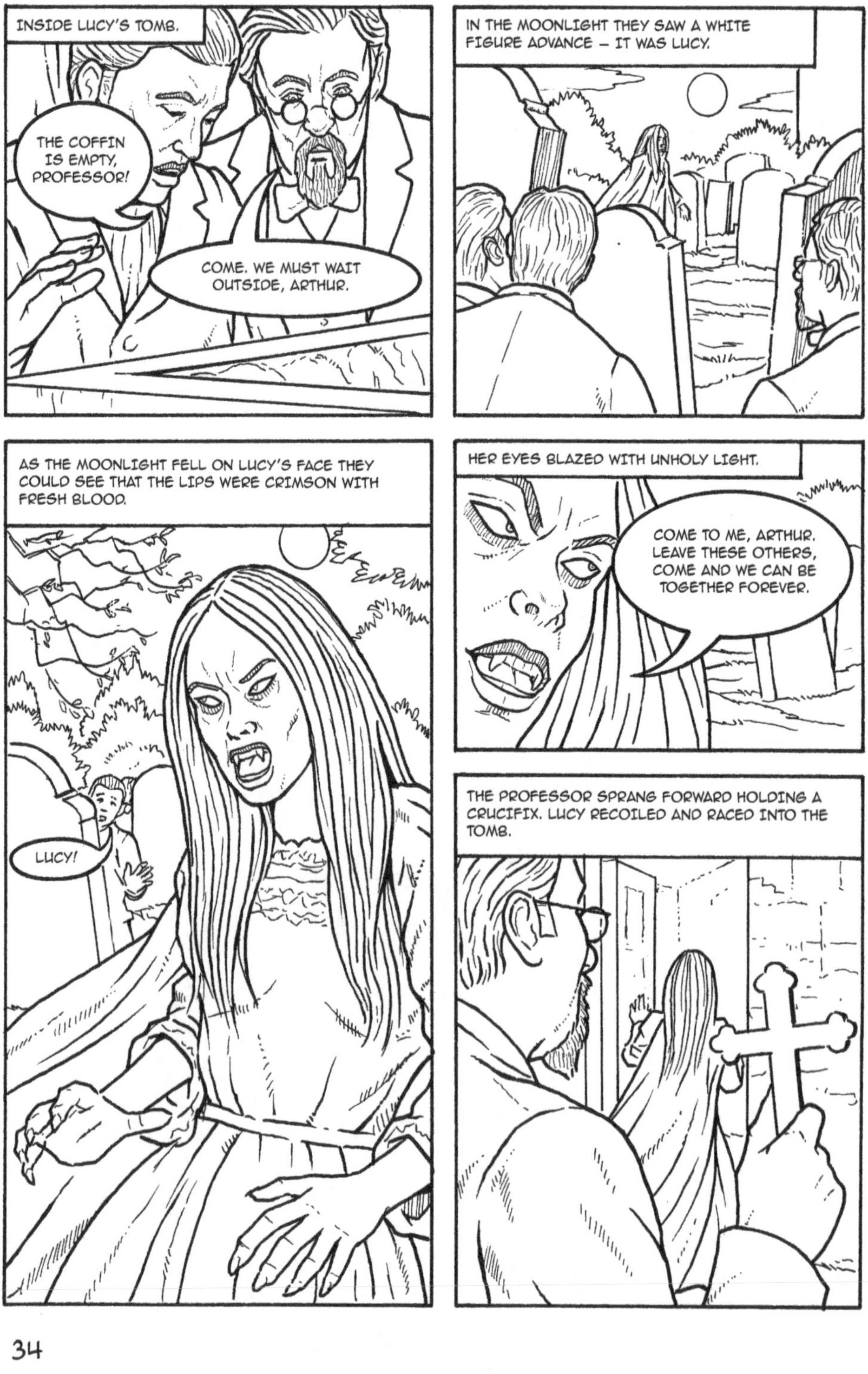
INSIDE LUCY'S TOMB.
THE COFFIN IS EMPTY, PROFESSOR!
COME. WE MUST WAIT OUTSIDE, ARTHUR.
IN THE MOONLIGHT THEY SAW A WHITE FIGURE ADVANCE – IT WAS LUCY.
AS THE MOONLIGHT FELL ON LUCY'S FACE THEY COULD SEE THAT THE LIPS WERE CRIMSON WITH FRESH BLOOD.
LUCY!
HER EYES BLAZED WITH UNHOLY LIGHT.
COME TO ME, ARTHUR. LEAVE THESE OTHERS, COME AND WE CAN BE TOGETHER FOREVER.
THE PROFESSOR SPRANG FORWARD HOLDING A CRUCIFIX. LUCY RECOILED AND RACED INTO THE TOMB.

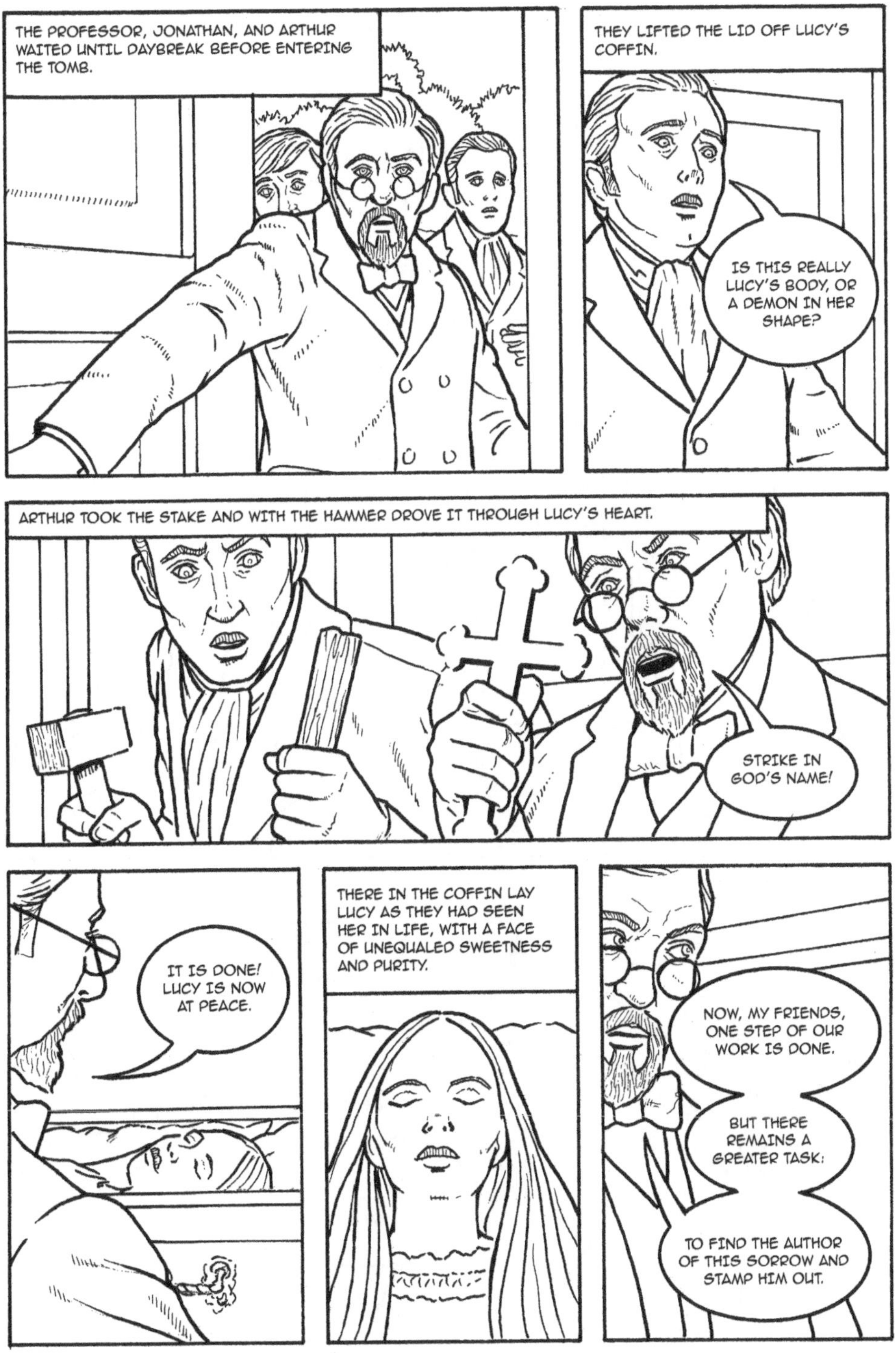
THE PROFESSOR, JONATHAN, AND ARTHUR WAITED UNTIL DAYBREAK BEFORE ENTERING THE TOMB.
THEY LIFTED THE LID OFF LUCY'S COFFIN.
IS THIS REALLY LUCY'S BODY, OR A DEMON IN HER SHAPE?
ARTHUR TOOK THE STAKE AND WITH THE HAMMER DROVE IT THROUGH LUCY'S HEART.
STRIKE IN GOD'S NAME!
IT IS DONE! LUCY IS NOW AT PEACE.
THERE IN THE COFFIN LAY LUCY AS THEY HAD SEEN HER IN LIFE, WITH A FACE OF UNEQUALED SWEETNESS AND PURITY.
NOW, MY FRIENDS, ONE STEP OF OUR WORK IS DONE.
BUT THERE REMAINS A GREATER TASK:
TO FIND THE AUTHOR OF THIS SORROW AND STAMP HIM OUT.

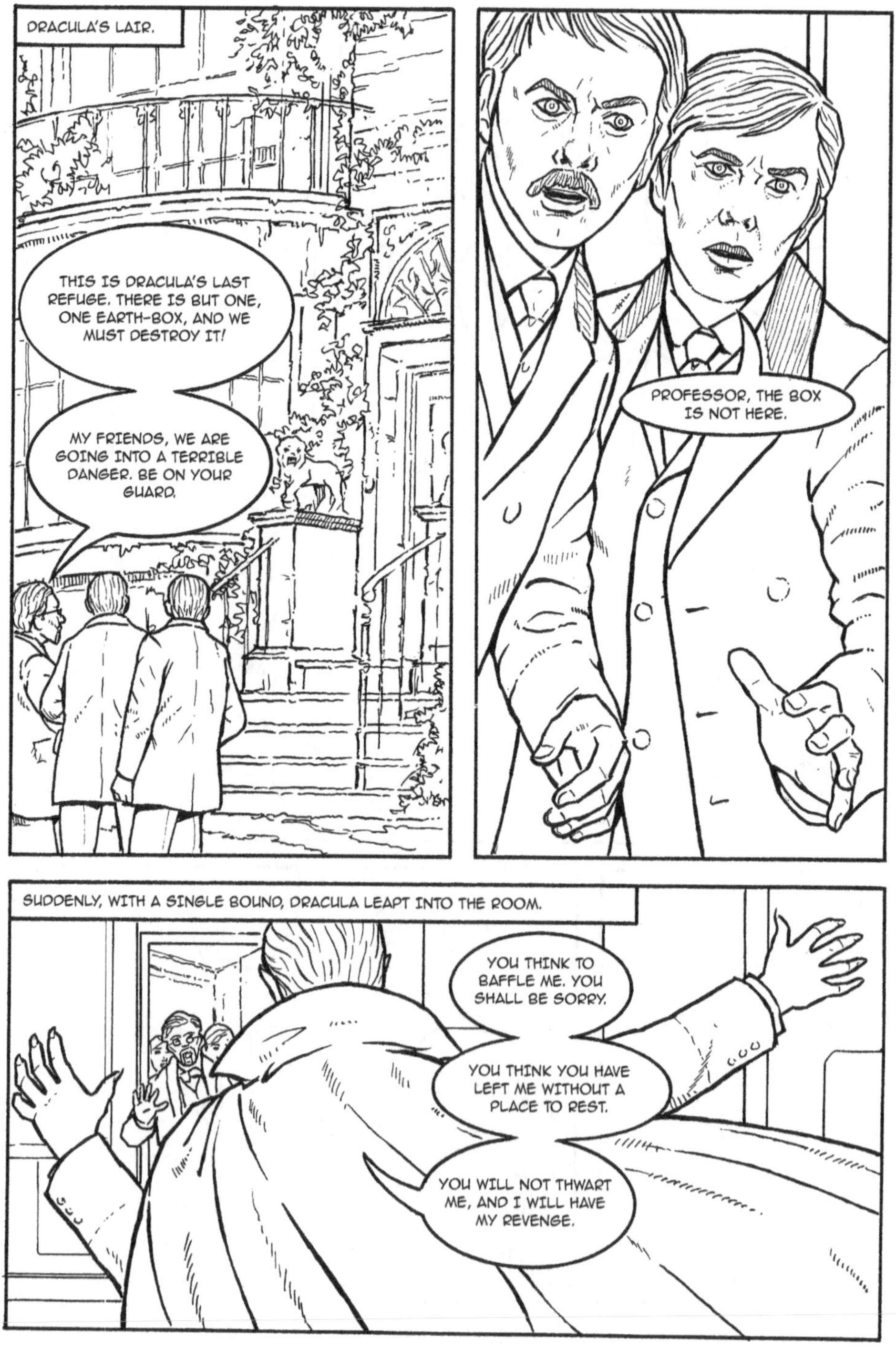
DRACULA'S LAIR.
THIS IS DRACULA'S LAST REFUGE. THERE IS BUT ONE, ONE EARTH-BOX, AND WE MUST DESTROY IT!
MY FRIENDS, WE ARE GOING INTO A TERRIBLE DANGER. BE ON YOUR GUARD.
PROFESSOR, THE BOX IS NOT HERE.
SUDDENLY, WITH A SINGLE BOUND, DRACULA LEAPT INTO THE ROOM.
YOU THINK TO BAFFLE ME. YOU SHALL BE SORRY.
YOU THINK YOU HAVE LEFT ME WITHOUT A PLACE TO REST.
YOU WILL NOT THWART ME, AND I WILL HAVE MY REVENGE.

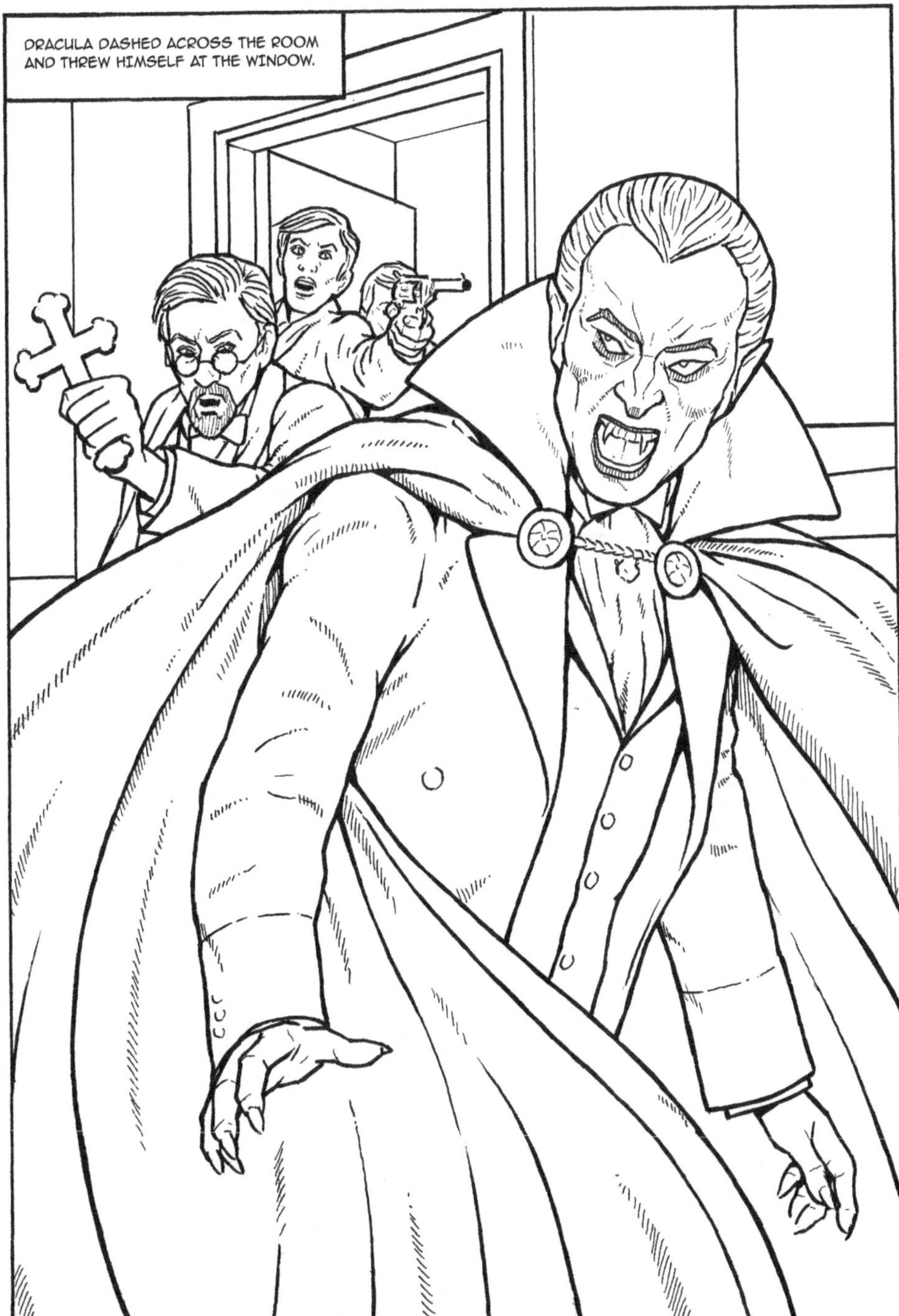
DRACULA DASHED ACROSS THE ROOM
AND THREW HIMSELF AT THE WINDOW.

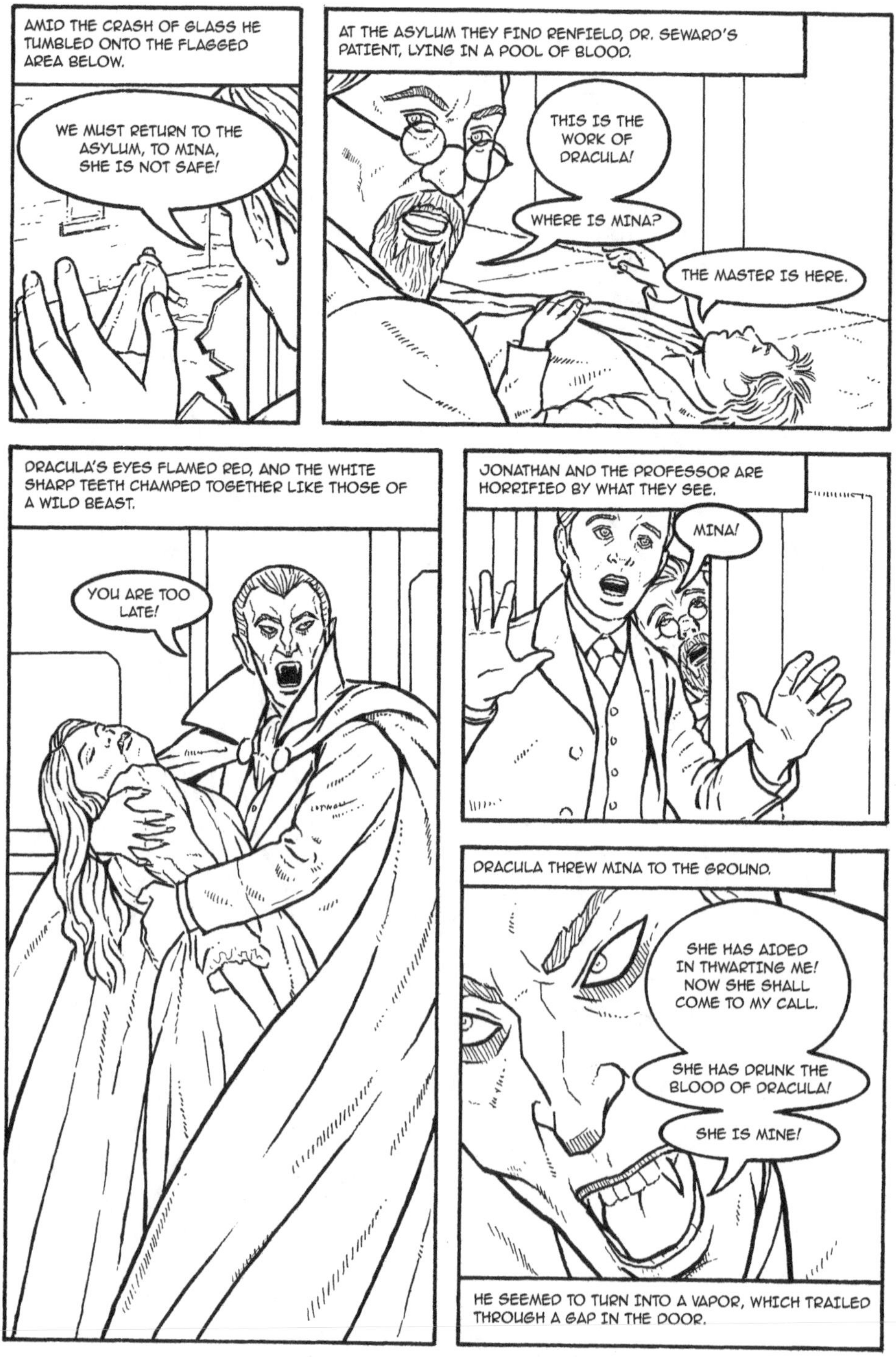
AMID THE CRASH OF GLASS HE TUMBLED ONTO THE FLAGGED AREA BELOW.
WE MUST RETURN TO THE ASYLUM, TO MINA, SHE IS NOT SAFE!
AT THE ASYLUM THEY FIND RENFIELD, DR. SEWARD'S PATIENT, LYING IN A POOL OF BLOOD.
THIS IS THE WORK OF DRACULA!
WHERE IS MINA?
THE MASTER IS HERE.
DRACULA'S EYES FLAMED RED, AND THE WHITE SHARP TEETH CHAMPED TOGETHER LIKE THOSE OF A WILD BEAST.
YOU ARE TOO LATE!
JONATHAN AND THE PROFESSOR ARE HORRIFIED BY WHAT THEY SEE.
MINA!
DRACULA THREW MINA TO THE GROUND.
SHE HAS AIDED IN THWARTING ME! NOW SHE SHALL COME TO MY CALL.
SHE HAS DRUNK THE BLOOD OF DRACULA!
SHE IS MINE!
HE SEEMED TO TURN INTO A VAPOR, WHICH TRAILED THROUGH A GAP IN THE DOOR.

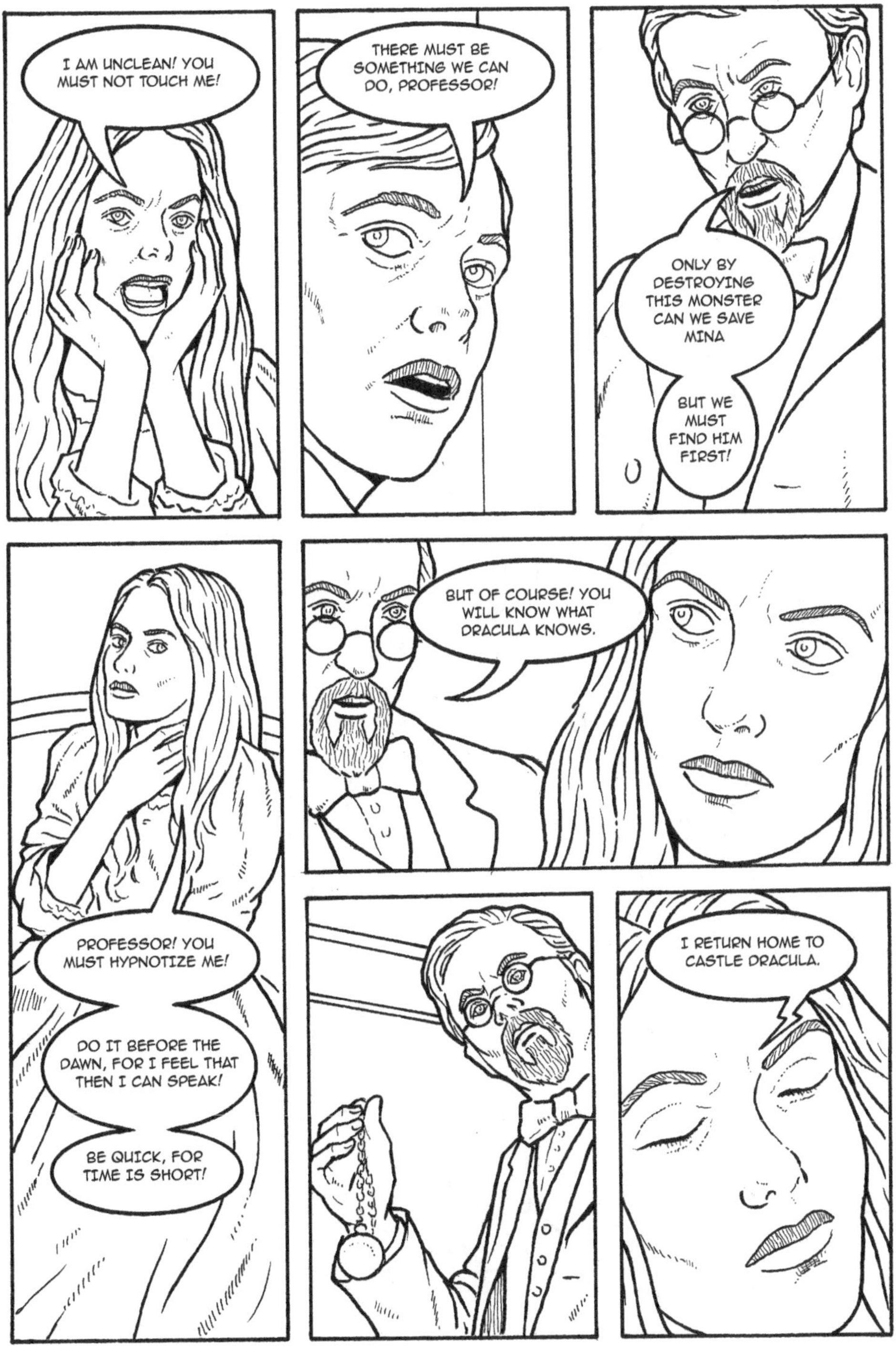
I AM UNCLEAN! YOU MUST NOT TOUCH ME!
THERE MUST BE SOMETHING WE CAN DO, PROFESSOR!
ONLY BY DESTROYING THIS MONSTER CAN WE SAVE MINA
BUT WE MUST FIND HIM FIRST!
PROFESSOR! YOU MUST HYPNOTIZE ME!
DO IT BEFORE THE DAWN, FOR I FEEL THAT THEN I CAN SPEAK!
BE QUICK, FOR TIME IS SHORT!
BUT OF COURSE! YOU WILL KNOW WHAT DRACULA KNOWS.
I RETURN HOME TO CASTLE DRACULA.

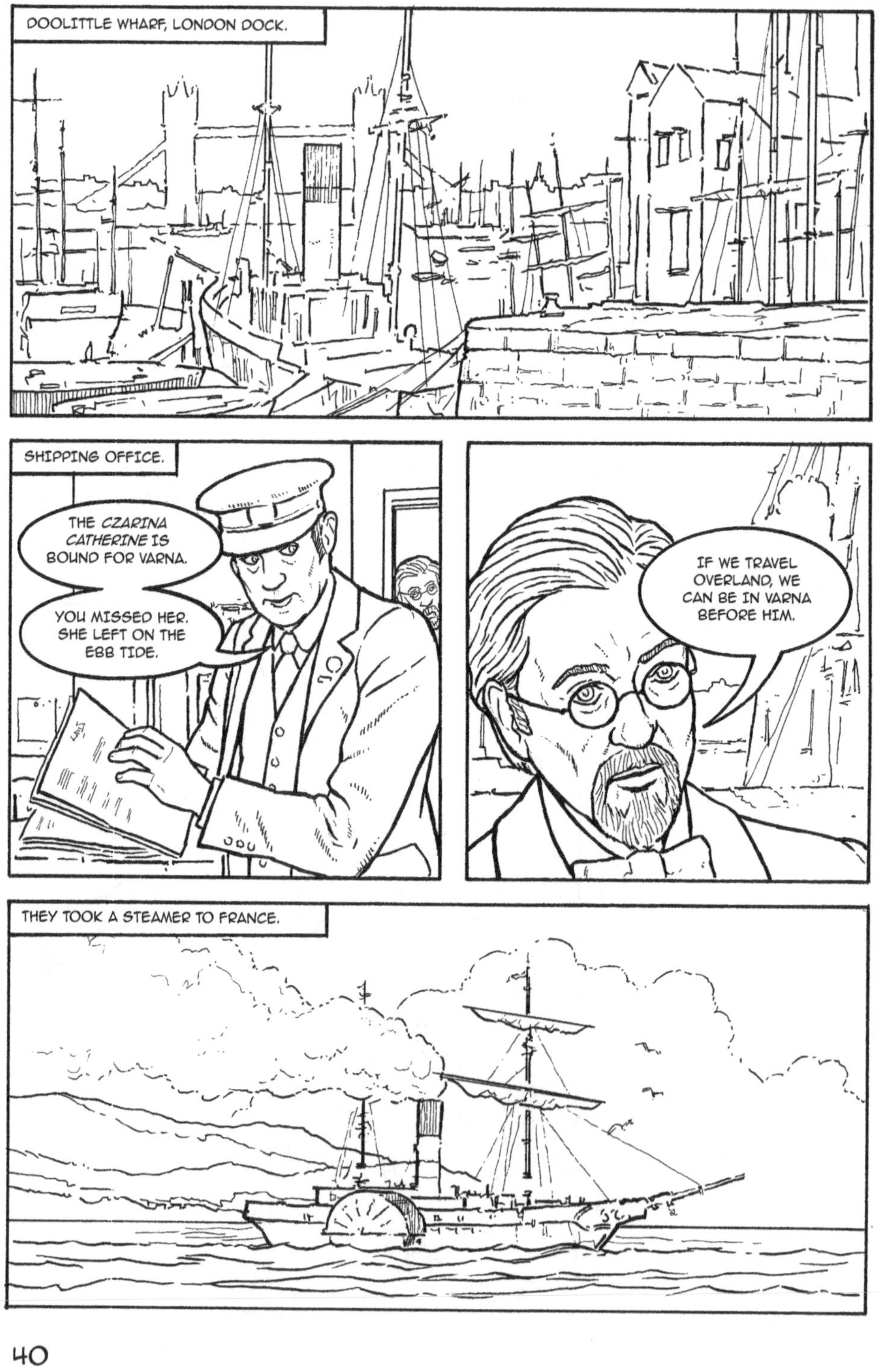
DOOLITTLE WHARF, LONDON DOCK.
SHIPPING OFFICE.
THE *CZARINA CATHERINE* IS BOUND FOR VARNA.
YOU MISSED HER. SHE LEFT ON THE EBB TIDE.
IF WE TRAVEL OVERLAND, WE CAN BE IN VARNA BEFORE HIM.
THEY TOOK A STEAMER TO FRANCE.

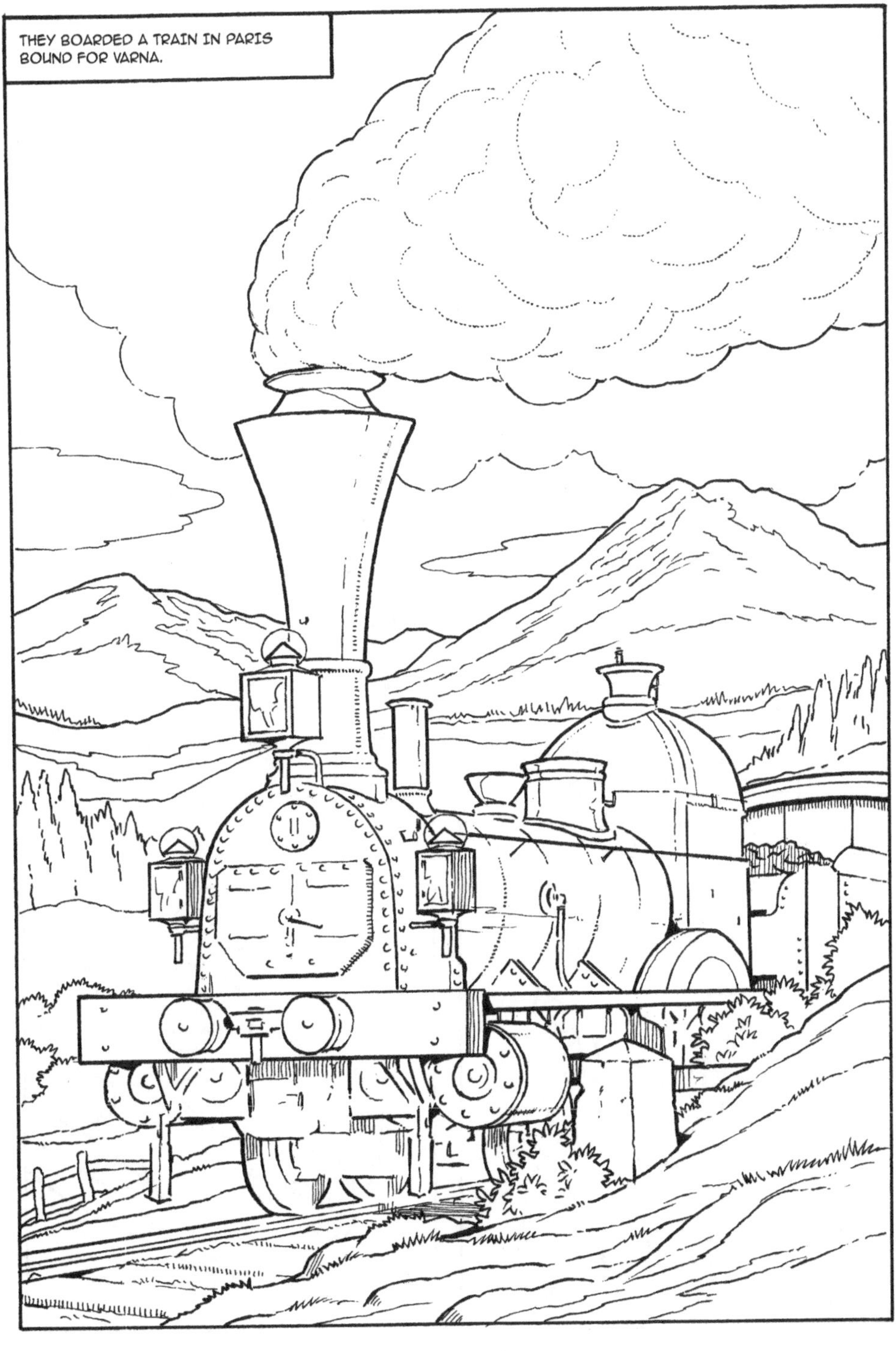
THEY BOARDED A TRAIN IN PARIS BOUND FOR VARNA.

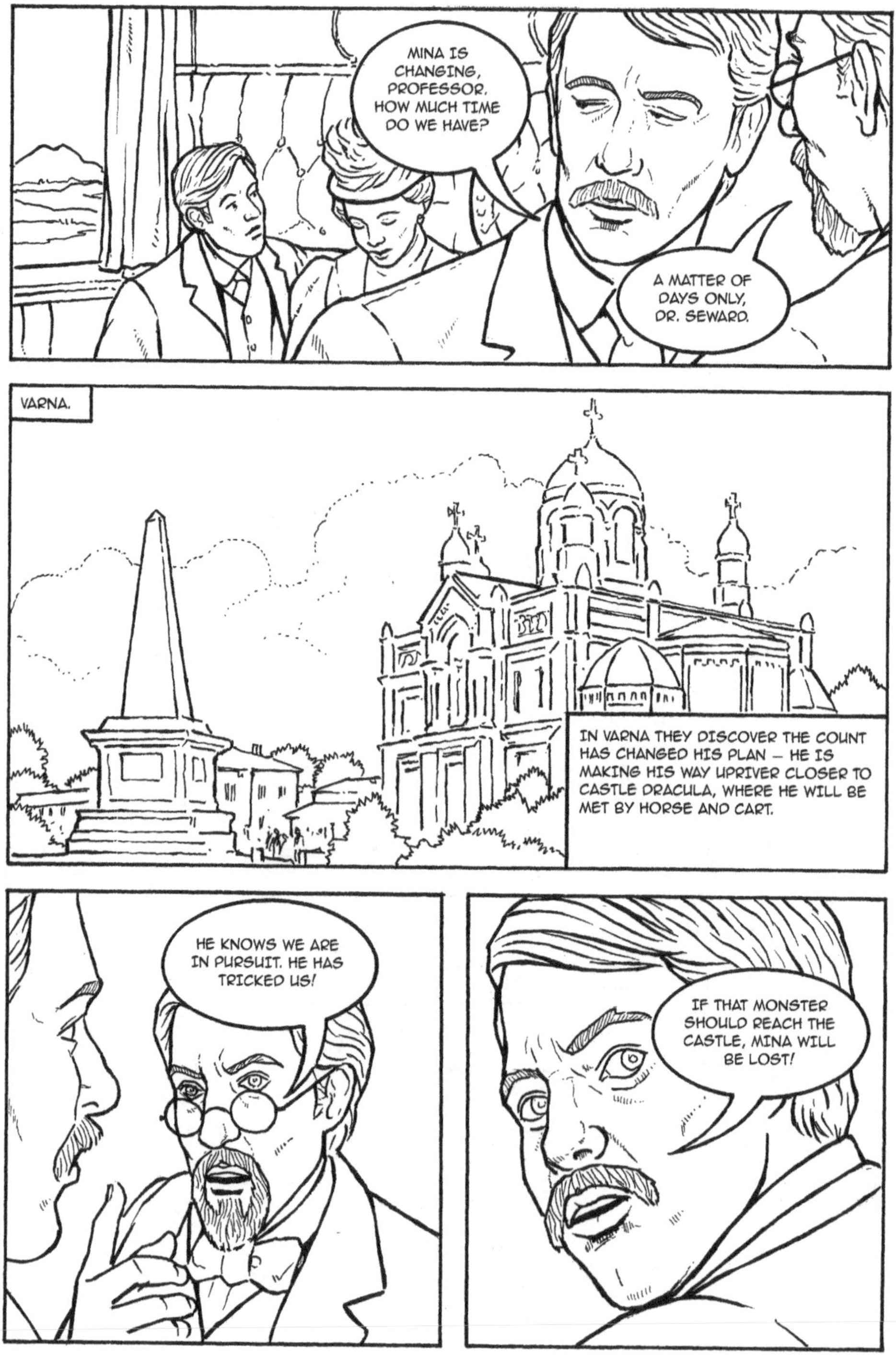
MINA IS CHANGING, PROFESSOR. HOW MUCH TIME DO WE HAVE?
A MATTER OF DAYS ONLY, DR. SEWARD.
VARNA.
IN VARNA THEY DISCOVER THE COUNT HAS CHANGED HIS PLAN — HE IS MAKING HIS WAY UPRIVER CLOSER TO CASTLE DRACULA, WHERE HE WILL BE MET BY HORSE AND CART.
HE KNOWS WE ARE IN PURSUIT. HE HAS TRICKED US!
IF THAT MONSTER SHOULD REACH THE CASTLE, MINA WILL BE LOST!

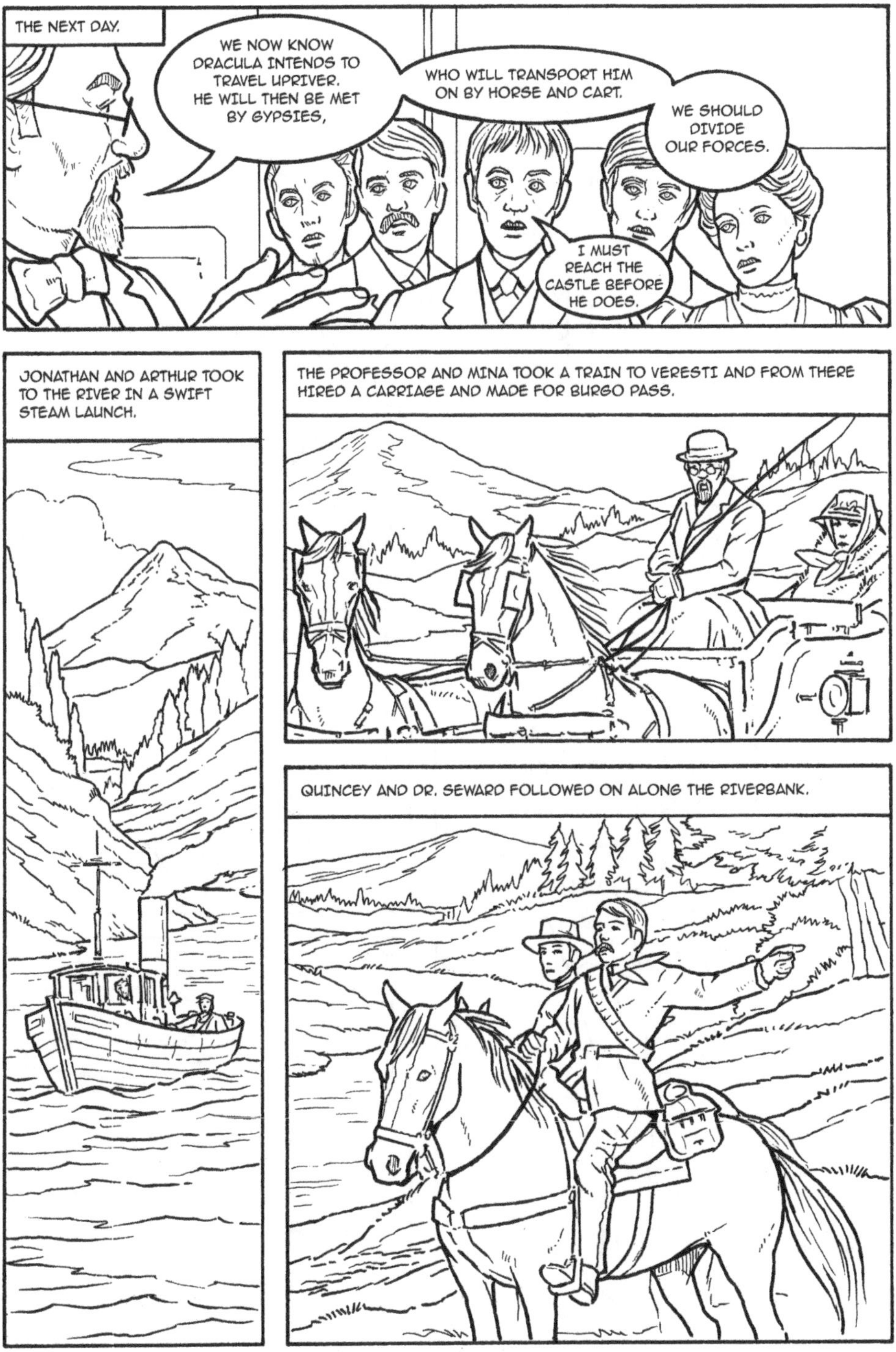
THE NEXT DAY.
WE NOW KNOW DRACULA INTENDS TO TRAVEL UPRIVER. HE WILL THEN BE MET BY GYPSIES,
WHO WILL TRANSPORT HIM ON BY HORSE AND CART.
WE SHOULD DIVIDE OUR FORCES.
I MUST REACH THE CASTLE BEFORE HE DOES.
JONATHAN AND ARTHUR TOOK TO THE RIVER IN A SWIFT STEAM LAUNCH.
THE PROFESSOR AND MINA TOOK A TRAIN TO VERESTI AND FROM THERE HIRED A CARRIAGE AND MADE FOR BURGO PASS.
QUINCEY AND DR. SEWARD FOLLOWED ON ALONG THE RIVERBANK.

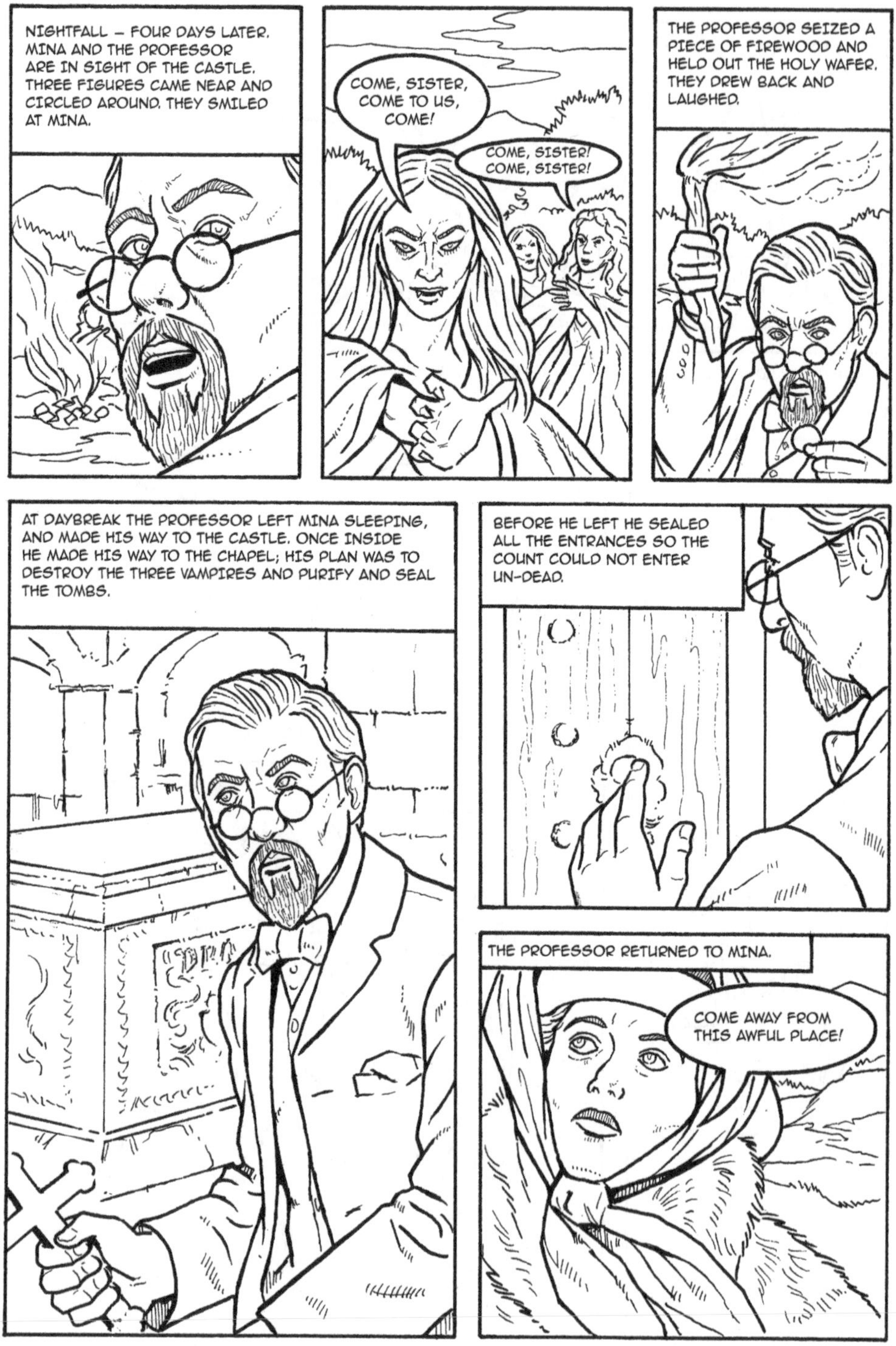
NIGHTFALL — FOUR DAYS LATER. MINA AND THE PROFESSOR ARE IN SIGHT OF THE CASTLE. THREE FIGURES CAME NEAR AND CIRCLED AROUND. THEY SMILED AT MINA.
COME, SISTER, COME TO US, COME!
COME, SISTER! COME, SISTER!
THE PROFESSOR SEIZED A PIECE OF FIREWOOD AND HELD OUT THE HOLY WAFER. THEY DREW BACK AND LAUGHED.
AT DAYBREAK THE PROFESSOR LEFT MINA SLEEPING, AND MADE HIS WAY TO THE CASTLE. ONCE INSIDE HE MADE HIS WAY TO THE CHAPEL; HIS PLAN WAS TO DESTROY THE THREE VAMPIRES AND PURIFY AND SEAL THE TOMBS.
BEFORE HE LEFT HE SEALED ALL THE ENTRANCES SO THE COUNT COULD NOT ENTER UN-DEAD.
THE PROFESSOR RETURNED TO MINA.
COME AWAY FROM THIS AWFUL PLACE!

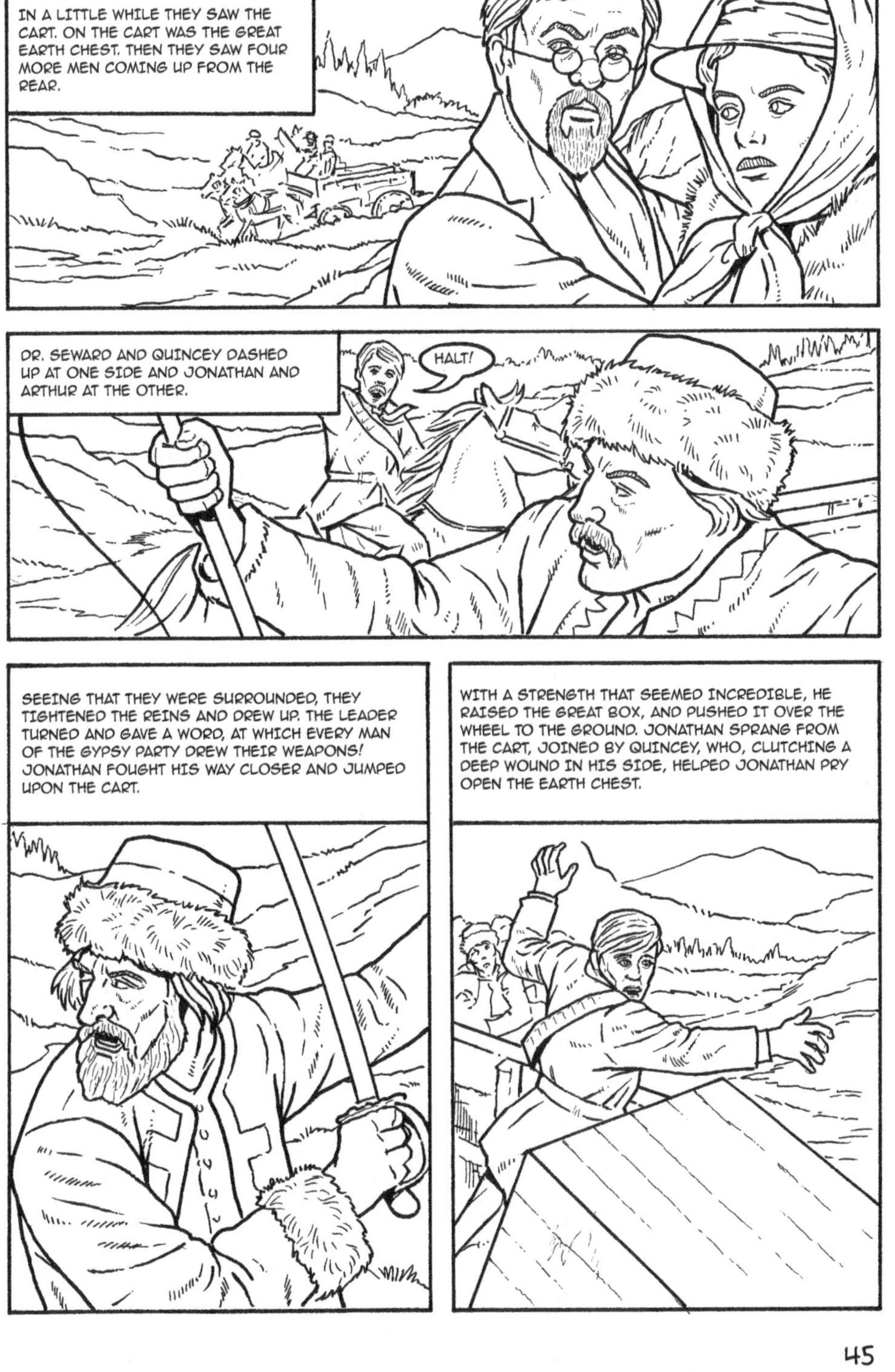
IN A LITTLE WHILE THEY SAW THE CART. ON THE CART WAS THE GREAT EARTH CHEST. THEN THEY SAW FOUR MORE MEN COMING UP FROM THE REAR.
DR. SEWARD AND QUINCEY DASHED UP AT ONE SIDE AND JONATHAN AND ARTHUR AT THE OTHER.
HALT!
SEEING THAT THEY WERE SURROUNDED, THEY TIGHTENED THE REINS AND DREW UP. THE LEADER TURNED AND GAVE A WORD, AT WHICH EVERY MAN OF THE GYPSY PARTY DREW THEIR WEAPONS! JONATHAN FOUGHT HIS WAY CLOSER AND JUMPED UPON THE CART.
WITH A STRENGTH THAT SEEMED INCREDIBLE, HE RAISED THE GREAT BOX, AND PUSHED IT OVER THE WHEEL TO THE GROUND. JONATHAN SPRANG FROM THE CART, JOINED BY QUINCEY, WHO, CLUTCHING A DEEP WOUND IN HIS SIDE, HELPED JONATHAN PRY OPEN THE EARTH CHEST.

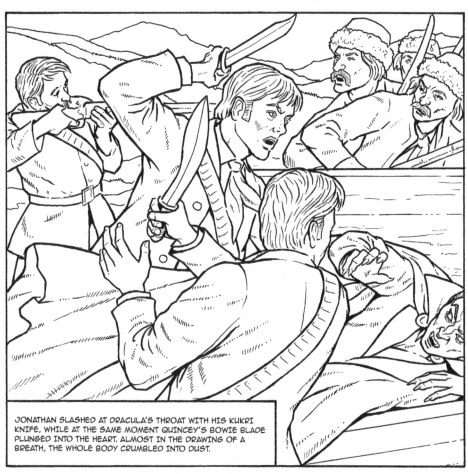

JONATHAN SLASHED AT DRACULA'S THROAT WITH HIS KUKRI KNIFE, WHILE AT THE SAME MOMENT QUINCEY'S BOWIE BLADE PLUNGED INTO THE HEART. ALMOST IN THE DRAWING OF A BREATH, THE WHOLE BODY CRUMBLED INTO DUST.

THE CURSE HAD PASSED AWAY.

THEY LOOKED BACK AND SAW THE CLEAR LINES OF THE CASTLE STANDING OUT AGAINST THE RAYS OF THE SETTING SUN.

THE END